PITY BEYOND ALL TELLING

James O'Halloran

Pity Beyond All Telling

AND OTHER SHORT STORIES AND ANECDOTES

the columba press

First edition, 2010, published by
the columba press
55A Spruce Avenue, Stillorgan Industrial Park,
Blackrock, Co Dublin

Cover by Bill Bolger
Cover picture by Marley Irish, www.artmarleyirish@yahoo.com
Origination by The Columba Press
Printed in Ireland by
Colour Books Ltd, Dublin

ISBN 978 1 85607 708 8

Copyright © 2010, James O'Halloran SDB

Contents

Introduction by Brendan Kennelly   7

LATIN AMERICAN DAYS

Eccentrics All	9
The Wall	15
Beyond Tears	16
The Least of These	19
The Pelican	22
The Dig Out	24
A Curious Sighting	28
Death, Where Is Thy Sting? I	31
Death, Where Is Thy Sting? II	32
Death, Where Is Thy Sting? III	34
Angry Fish	35
Home Thoughts from Abroad	38
Not Our World	41
A Lesson in Love	45
Candy for the Kids	47

AFRICAN DAYS

God Is a Catholic	52
Music and Dissonance	59
Stella	63
Moonstruck	67
The Sun Sets	69
Discovery	76
The Vulture	80
Heart in Hand	82
It's the Tears of Things	88
An Unfortunate Error	94
The Cotton Tree	97
Shark	100
Good News	102

Saving the Fish from Drowning	104
Christopher, I Owe You	105
Land of Neutral Faces	107

AVONREE DAYS

The Hedgehog	111
Jerusalem, Jerusalem	114
Interlude	118
Dads' Army	120
So Passes Worldly Glory	124
Ghosts I	125
Ghosts II	130
Ghosts III	132
The Miracle	133
Nostalgia	135
Little Unremembered Acts	140
The Road Less Travelled	142
A Near Thing	147
Waiting for Kathleen	148
Incident by the Somme	155
Out of this World	158
Weaver of Yarns	161
Pity Beyond All Telling	164

OTHER DAYS

Callers	178
Daddy, Daddy	181
Rachel	185
A Dire Decision	187
Go Not Gently	188
Phew!	190
Brush with Greatness I	191
Brush with Greatness II	195
Brush with Greatness III	197
Brush with Greatness IV	199
The Bagman	205
In Search of José Marins	207
Rendezvous	208
Tomorrow is Another Day	210

Introduction

Jim O'Halloran's stories are moving and authentic. He writes out of his own experience, which is rich and deep. He writes with a shrewd eye and an accurate ear, catching and holding the reader's attention with some startlingly precise images and with dialogue so natural and accurate the reader feels at times as if he were eavesdropping on the characters of these tales.

The two qualities in Jim O'Halloran's writing which I find impressive are his compassion and his humour. His compassion, his fluent, deep, instinctive feeling of loving sympathy for others, is present in all his stories, not only in the stories about people, but in the stories about other creatures great and small.

His humour is like a warm, heartening presence breathing life and insight into his prose. It is present in his observations, in his moments of solitude, in his convincing dialogue (see especially 'Eccentrics All') and in his calm, tolerant acceptance of finite human frailty in all its infinite variety.

Some of these stories have the conciseness and universality of parables. They do not moralise; but by being deeply and personally imaginative they make the reader think about the strange recesses of his own moral nature.

This is a skilled and stimulating collection by a gifted writer who also has the good fortune to be a fine human being. I am personally grateful for this fact. Readers of this rich and vigorous book will, I believe, experience a similar gratitude.

Brendan Kennelly
Trinity College, Dublin

Latin American Days

Eccentrics All

I had only two encounters with Padre José Larumbe in my life, but each is etched graphically on my mind.

The first time was when I was walking down a long empty corridor in a Latin American monastery that went back to the time of the conquistadores. The silence was broken only by the ancient boards complaining beneath my feet. From an ascetic whitewashed wall a gaunt St John of the Cross looked heavenwards with large liquid eyes from a fading and fraying oil painting. On his desk was a grinning skull.

Not far from this picture there was a similar one of John's fellow reformer, Teresa of Avila. With a no-nonsense look and raised forefinger she seemed to be admonishing her sisters to pull up their socks; or rather to dispense with socks and shoes altogether and resort to sandals. Now this penchant for airy sandals which Teresa and John shared was one thing in the torrid Spanish summers, yet quite another in the nippy Spanish winters. And it certainly was not to be emulated in the Andes, where raw air can gnaw wild-eyed and mercilessly at unprotected toes.

As I pondered the 'eccentricities' of John and Teresa, a door burst open. Out came an elderly priest, as gaunt as John and as bald as his pet skull.

'What's your name?' he asked emphatically.

I told him.

'You're a gringo. Are you a priest?'

'Yes.'

'Secular or regular?'

'A Salesian.'

'Ah, St John Bosco! Great man ... Where do you come from?'

'Ireland.'

'North or South?'

'South.'

'Is that the part the English are occupying?'

'No.'

'Ah, so you're from *Irlanda la católica* ... O'Connell, San Patricio, De Valera, Bernardo O'Higgins, Mateo Talbot, Blessed Oliver Cromwell –'

'Plunkett,' I interposed.

'Wonderful nation *Irlanda*. I've read a lot about it. De Valera is a Spanish name, you know ... Spanish father ... And I wish our Indians would imitate the sobriety of your Mateo Talbot. But their bodies bestrew the gutters every weekend ... Wait a minute.'

He disappeared into his room, abandoning me like a spare wheel in the corridor.

'Down with the gringos!' he croaked from inside.

'Well that's a bit much,' I thought indignantly. 'This man isn't exactly a diplomat and me a gringo.' I was about to march off in a huff.

'Shut up, you stupid bird!'

So that was the explanation.

'Say Otero Romero ... Otero Romero ...'

'Oh no!' I groaned. 'Not another Otero Romero fanatic.'

Otero Romero was President of Ohiggania in the 1890s and governed the place like a blackthorn-wielding parish priest. He would even sally forth at night and chase courting couples from the walls of the Presidential Palace. These promptly escaped to the shadows of the neighbouring cathedral. His memory was revered by priests of a certain age, but the younger ones thought him 'a silly old geyser'.

'Otero Romero,' muttered the bird as though under protest.

'That's better.'

The priest reappeared with a pile of books. 'Take these. Spread the word. It's the life of Otero Romero. The whole world should know about this man. In fact he's more appreciated in some places abroad than here at home. His name is a household word in France. By the way, you're from?'

'Ireland.'

'Ah, *Irlanda la católica!* De Valera, San Patricio, Bernardo

O'Higgins, O'Connell, Mateo Talbot, Blessed Oliver Cromwell –'
'Plunkett.'
'Send these to Ireland – airmail.'
'But they're in Spanish, father.'
'Then translate the book and do a signal service to humanity ... I wrote it myself. Here's the name ... José Larumbe.'
'José Larumbe,' I repeated. 'It has a lilt to it.'
The door of his room had slowly groaned open, and I noticed that his shelves were packed with spare copies of the work. I also saw the mynah-bird regarding me warily with cocked beady eye.
'Don't waste a minute. Go and spread the word.'
'*Gringo loco!*' croaked the bird most inopportunely and blew a raspberry.
'*Dios mio,* what's come over that bird? Who could possibly have taught him to be so rude?' asked José lamely. 'Anyway, you're Irish and Catholic ... not really a gringo ... The English and *yanquis* are the real gringos. Unfortunately most people don't make the distinction. They lump all English speakers together and call them gringos. But the Irish are different ... a great people. Didn't De Valera do well to overcome the drink?'
'Yes, marvellously,' I replied with resignation, as I gave up trying to unsnarl Padre José's Irish history.
'He could serve as a shining example for our Indians.'
Then as suddenly as he had appeared, José disappeared into his room. 'Say Otero Romero ... Otero Romero ...' he called from behind closed doors.
I stood at a loss with the bundle of books and raised my eyes to heaven. I looked to John of the Cross. His eyes were also raised to heaven.
'Listen, John,' I murmured, 'if you and Tess were eccentrics, you're certainly in the right corridor.' And I set out to find a suitable place in which to dump my pile of books, while thanking God that I hadn't met one Padre Lopez, who also lived in that monastery and had written eight volumes of fact, fiction and pious hearsay about Otero Romero. And he said there were still a few volumes to go 'if God spares me.' But, 'tis rumoured, God is merciful.

Walking between the colonnades that bordered the peaceful monastery garden, I met a silver-haired priest saying his office as palms waved and chortling doves bowed their adoration to one another by the softly splashing fountain in the middle of the area. Looking momentarily at me and the books, he gave a harsh little laugh. 'I see you ran into old Larumbe,' he muttered ironically. 'You'll find a bin for garbage on the way out.' He then went back to devotedly reading his office. 'Waste Paper' announced the bin rather more gently.

* * *

Next time I met Padre José Larumbe was in the Church of St Cajetan, adjacent to his monastery, when I wandered in to say a few prayers. That church I loved because it was the people's church, a favourite haunt of Indians from the countryside. With downtrodden looks they padded in on bare or sandalled feet, lit their flickering stars of hope and placed them before *Jesus del Gran Poder*. His feet were also bare and the shoulders oppressed beneath the cross. He was a brother in the struggle.

A mother knelt with her son, a young man in his twenties. He had the sturdy black hair peculiar to his race, yet the face and hands were unusually refined and the dark eyes shone brightly. There was only the remotest hint of the bronzed, craggy-faced Inca. What a transformation consumption can work. The concerned mother rubbed him all over with a blessed candle before lighting it at the shrine of Christ. On the way out she would give him a drink of Cajetan's water under the benign purveyance of the saint.

In this church I always felt my soul distend and rest in the atmosphere of winking candles and sanctuary lamps that softly shed their crimson light.

Outside a confessional a little knot of people had gathered, obviously awaiting a priest. I placed my face in my hands and my mind gradually drifted. As always I recalled the Friary Chapel in my home town. I could hear the hobnail boots resound on the dusty wooden floor. As a four-year-old I used to kneel beside Grandad as Father Frost gave out the rosary. 'Hail Mary, full of grace, the Lord is with thee, blessed art thou among women and blessed is – 'Hoooly Mary, Mother of God...' the response swelled before he could finish. Then came the litany. 'Ark of the Covenant ... Gate of Heaven ... Morning Star ... ' To which the people replied encouragingly – and I joined them – 'Pray Frost'; or so at least it sounded to my childish ears. I smiled at the recollection. No matter how many years one has been away, in the depths of one's being there is always the faintest chick cheep of an aching for home.

The sudden click of a confessional door aroused me from my reverie. I looked up. A priest was entering. None other than Padre José Larumbe. Since he didn't have the indiscreet mynah bird perched on his shoulder, I thought I'd risk confession. Not that I find confession an easy chore or go to any old body, yet José had been pleasant enough (and certainly generous!) to me when last we met. True, he was a trifle odd, but isn't the litany of the saints peppered with glorious eccentrics?

I took my position outside the confessional. Nobody was moving. It was as though all were waiting for someone to try the water. An old woman with a translucent lantern-jawed face glanced at me fleetingly with dark wells of sanctity and then pulled a shawl over her frosty head.

Padre José murmured a blessing, then asked, 'How long since your last confession?' A mite loud I felt, but since I wasn't as yet indicting myself, I let it pass.

'Two months. And bless me father for I have sinned. I am a priest and a religious.'

'A priest and a religious and you haven't been to confession for two months ... umph ... Anyway, how many times?' he shouted.

Outside a woman, either decent or scrupulous, had a prolonged spasm of coughing and lengthily blew her nose.

'How many times what, father?'

'How many times did you sin?' José was nothing if not to the point – and he was still shouting.

Dios mio, I must do something about this, I agonised. 'Father, you're embarrassing me,' I whispered hoarsely.

'WELL WHY DO YOU SIN THEN IF YOU'RE EMBARRASSED?'

I peered through the grille. So this was where the word 'grilling' had its origin?

'How many times?' loudly persisted my interrogator. And it was then that I saw him put something to his ear.

'Oh no,' I squirmed, 'an ear-trumpet. This is a nightmare. I'm caught in a time warp ... last century. Maybe he found all those lives of Otero Romero at the bottom of the dustbin.' Without another word I upped and fled.

Nobody stirred to replace me. In flight I caught a man's bemused glance, which seemed to suggest that I could read the signs of the heavens but not the signs of the times. Anyway, I took to my heels leaving José with the trumpet to his ear.

For all I know he may still be there. Indeed over the years I have often had visions of him frozen in that posture, awaiting the last trumpet when he will be summoned to the Valley of Jehoshaphat with Otero Romero (scattering courting couples on the way), San Patricio, De Valera, O'Connell, Bernardo O'Higgins, Mateo Talbot and Blessed Oliver Cromwell – ooops! – Plunkett! An eccentric Padre José certainly was, but was I any different? That was the question.

The Wall

Thirty million people would die of hunger that year. So the Teacher said. And while thirty million were dying of hunger more than one million dollars would be spent on armaments that could annihilate the human race. If the manufacture of those horrendous weapons was halted for only two weeks each year, the basic food and medical problems of the world could be solved for the entire year.

The dark young eyes of his audience flashed with indignation. What the Teacher was saying was for them only too real, because the spectral people around them were daily stalked by cruel hunger and immature death. Indeed they themselves knew the pangs of want. But they felt hopeless in the face of this overwhelming problem.

The Teacher went to the blackboard and slowly started to draw. When he finished, there was the picture of a massive forbidding wall.

'Tell me,' he said to the young people, 'do you sacrifice yourselves in any way for your deprived brothers and sisters?'

'Well,' began Marcelo tentatively, 'I teach in a night-school for illiterates.' The Teacher put a tiny crack in the obscene wall.

'I help in a dispensary at weekends,' said René. Another tiny crack.

'And I try to counsel small kids who sniff glue,' chimed in Adriana. Still a further crack.

Narcisa ran a club for children, Mario a magazine for his area, and Pedro organised summer camps. The Teacher went on drawing.

'Suppose,' he said, 'enough plain people all over the world, through their acts of significant sharing, go on making tiny flaws in this great monolith of selfishness, what will become of the wall?'

Hope dawned in their eyes.

Beyond Tears

An air of foreboding hung over the tiny mud-floored home of the Jumipanta family. The father, José, and six children sat breakfasting on black coffee and dry bread, while the mother, Yolanda, huddled near an oil stove, for it was bleak, with the one-year-old Manuelito upon her knee.

The six children at the table sensed something strange and, over the rims of their enamel mugs, anxiously searched the faces of their parents with great dark eyes.

Juan and Maria Taipe called on their way to work. Juan had the rope of the cargador looped over his shoulder (he would labour in the marketplace through the long day, like a beast of burden) and Maria had some cooked beans that she would hopefully sell, if only for a pittance.

'Today is the day?' inquired Juan.

'It is so,' replied José.

'I feel it.'

'Thank you, Juan.'

'There's no other remedy.'

'Tis the will of God.'

'It is so.'

'Such is the life of the poor.'

Juan and Maria then patted the baby on the head and went their way.

For a long time, José and Yolanda froze in Indian stoicism.

'Will we send the children out?' asked Yolanda.

'No, my love. They must always remember how hard it was for you and for me. They must share our suffering.'

The sharp-eared children looked on wonderingly.

After what seemed an eternity, there was the sound of an approaching car.

José looked out. A blue Mercedes was ascending the steep dirt road scattering scrawny chickens and wretched pigs noisily in its wake. Skeletal dogs moved lethargically from its wheels when death seemed imminent. The vehicle halted outside the Jumipanta home. A pair of gringos, husband and wife, got out.

'Good day. How are you?' they greeted the family, their North American accent coming through the Spanish.

'We are well, to God be thanks,' replied José.

The gringo then conversed with his wife in English. 'There's no point in dragging this out, honey. It's bad enough without dragging it out.'

'I agree.'

'The baby is a sorry sight.'

'Wait till you see what a bath and shampoo will do. That dark hair will come up shining and silky. Then we'll deck him out in some nice clothes.'

The gringo went towards José, put a not unkindly hand on his shoulder and handed him a bulging envelope. 'This will help. Don't worry. Manuelito will have a better life.'

His wife then took the baby from the now trembling arms of Yolanda, whose face bore an expression of infinite, if impassive, pain.

They all trooped out to the car. Eleven-year-old Pablo, the eldest child, sensed that something was gravely amiss. A quiet tear edged down his cheek. The second eldest, Margarita, looked curiously into his face and sidled close to him. '*Adios*,' shouted the gringos and waved their hands. The lady caught Manuelito's tiny arm and helped him to wave goodbye. The car departed in a cloud of dust and the little fellow looked into his mother's face with consternation as he sped away to 'a better life'.

For what seemed an age, the family remained rooted to the spot, a silent tableaux. 'Let's go inside,' said José at last.

Listlessly, Yolanda poured out the remains of the morning coffee. They drank it slowly and without joy. José looked sadly at the children. 'You can go up the mountain and pick some alfalfa for the donkey.' This they loved to do, yet today they went silently, like a small funeral procession.

Outside the weather was overcast and misty. Low-lying clouds garlanded the sullen Andes. It was doubtful if the sun would show its face. José and Yolanda sat huddled, wordlessly, near the oil stove.

Eventually José stood up, took some money from the envelope, threw the remainder in disgust on the floor and stalked out.

It was night when he returned – hopelessly drunk.

'Coffee!' he demanded in a thick truculent voice.

'I'll prepare some,' said Yolanda quietly.

'Prepare!' he shouted. 'Daughter of a bitch ... It should be ready ... I want it now, now!' He set upon his wife and began to rain blows upon her. The awakened children lay petrified in their beds.

José rushed headlong out into the darkness. Yolanda turned to Pablo. 'Pablo, lock the door after me. Look after the house and the children.'

'Yes Mamma.'

She followed her husband as he stumbled blindly through the night. Spent at last, he crumbled to the cheerless earth and wept bitterly.

'My love, I had to do it. If I didn't we'd all starve.'

'Hush, hush, I know,' she replied.

'I'm sorry.' Still sobbing, he mercifully fell asleep. Back home the children too cried themselves to sleep.

And Yolanda, with breaking heart, stayed by her man during the long dark hours.

The Least of These

The meeting of the basic community was over, and most of the members had scurried to their nearby houses. I sat in the humble living room of the Chavez family, waiting for the weather to clear. Present also was Rosita, an eighteen-year-old girl with auburn hair, soft features and the deepest and most concerned eyes you ever saw. Outside the lightning momentarily shattered the skies, thunder rolled long and resonantly among the Andes and the rain assaulted the earth with tropical fury.

The living room was a determined if pathetic effort to create a semblance of respectability. There was a glaring red sofa covered with preservative plastic and a few ill-assorted chairs. On one wall was a mirror, which created an illusion of amplitude, and from another the Dolorosa looked forlornly down from behind some plastic flowers. Here and there the wallpaper showed black blotches of dampness and was beginning to peel away. Through a door that opened on to a small yard there came the nauseating smell of stagnant slime from an open drain.

Off the living room there was a pokey, windowless kitchen. I could hear the *cuis* darting about there, chasing each other in their own dried excrement – people believed that this bedding somehow helped the fattening process – and emitting the short, sharp cooee sound from which these guinea-pigs got their name. A shaft of dusty light from some aperture in the roof revealed a few piebald mugs and plates with chipping enamel arranged on a crude shelf.

In this situation of enforced intimacy, Rosita chatted away freely.

Tired after our meeting, I listened with half an ear. She rhapsodised about the fun she had had at school and about the occasional trips up the slopes of the Andes to fly kites in the summer skies. Treasured were those moments when in a quiet corner she shared yearnings with her little friends. Of course, she said, school was everything to her; unlike her, the friends had homes to go to.

I pricked up my ears. Did she not have a home to go to?

While she was still little, she said, her father had given her away to an engineer and his family. Given her away ... I tried to absorb the enormity of it and looked closely at her face, which betrayed no signs of feeling. She was just carrying on matter of factly.

Had she been well treated in her new 'home'? Not so. As a tender girl she was just a slave at the beck and call of everyone and was abused by the boys in the family. On this I didn't ask her to elaborate. The meaning was only too sad and too clear.

'The engineer did send me to primary school. I suppose he felt he was doing a lot for me really.'

Anger and indignation were beginning to smoulder like lava in my heart against the insensitive engineer and against Rosita's father, whom I knew. By that time, at least, the father had become a very church-involved man, who moralised at meetings and would utter a bidding-prayer in a deep resonant voice at the drop of a hat. Short and powerful, with a barrel chest and bald pate ringed by jet black hair that flowed down into a flourishing beard, he looked like those biblical figures that you see on a bas-relief. If it weren't for the smiling dentures, he was my idea of what a Corinthian must have been like in Pauline times. But in the wake of Rosita's story, I thought of him simply as a hypocrite.

Having subsided inwardly, and noting the stoicism in Rosita's face, I decided that her unawareness had to be delicately handled. I felt that with consummate psychological tact she should be helped to cope with the corroding bitterness which must surely be suppressed deeply within her.

Tentatively, I asked how she felt about what her father had done.

'Oh well ... he was poor and probably couldn't help it. We were many children. He couldn't feed us all, so he gave me away.'

Why her?

'I suppose it was because I was the youngest. I wouldn't feel it as bad as the others. I didn't have the sense.'

But why did her father have to have so many children in the first place?

'Lots of children die as babies or soon after. Maybe he was afraid that he would be left without children when he got old. He'd have no one to look after him.'

All my presuppositions lay in ruins. I had much to learn about the oppressed.

The storm had passed and there was only the heavy dripping and splashing of water from the roof into puddles beneath the eaves. A scrawny dog lapped up water from one of them. I drove Rosita back to the opulent home to the north of Santo Domingo where she was now a skivvy. I shook her hand, kissed her lightly on the cheek, and said thanks. She looked at me a little surprised. 'Thanks to you, not me, for driving me back.'

The door of the house was thrown open and a beam of light challenged the darkness.

'What the hell kept you?' asked a harsh unfeeling voice. The door closed behind her and the light was no more. At the end of the month she would receive her eight dollars, for Rosita was no longer a slave but a hired servant.

The Pelican

Near the Pacific coastline shoals of tiny gleaming fishes gambolled and fed, blissfully unaware of the flock of pelicans which flapped along gently overhead in V formation, their eyes riveted on the steely waters below. Suddenly there was a glancing flash of silver near the crest of a wave and a pelican shot headlong upon its prey. The fish narrowly escaped the thrusting beak and scurried panic-stricken beneath a rock, shaking a nebulous galaxy of gold in its wake.

The frustrated pelican rode the waves for a moment and then spread her wings to take flight. Pain yelled through her right wing. She gave a little cry of agony. Again she flapped her wings in a vain attempt to rise; once more there was the excruciating pain. Terrified she sank back into the water. Her recklessly courageous dive had broken the wing on the sharp edge of a wave.

Pitying the bird, I approached to help. With racing heart she swam away from the shore to the safety of deeper waters. Locked forever in some remote corner of her brain was the image of a boy wantonly shooting her partner, who then floundered agonisingly in the sea but lay still at last as the water turned to crimson all around him.

For long hours she fought the swing of the ocean. The debilitating wing, however, took its toll and the tide gradually edged the ruffled bird, exhausted, on to the beach.

As I gazed at the light-ochre evening reflected dreamlike in the vast canvas of the ocean, I sighted her once more, a tiny dot on an endless strand. Out of her element, she was plodding laboriously along.

While she forged relentlessly onward, it did not occur to me that she could have any particular destination in view. But far up the beach, on a finger of sand left protruding into the Pacific by the receding tide, her companions stood huddled against the terrors of the encroaching night. It couldn't possibly be that she, a maimed pelican, was trying to reach them.

As the minutes passed, though, I realised that to reach them was precisely what she wanted to do. I became totally absorbed as the little drama unfolded. Would she make it?

The bird inched along, blinded by pain, in a seemingly hopeless struggle against distance and darkness. How she must have felt like bedding down on the inviting sand and drifting away into forgetfulness. From time to time there were the little cries of complaint against her fate. Gliding over the sands to join her friends would formerly have been a small matter. Nevertheless she persevered in her effort and, after what seemed an age, that perseverance was rewarded, for only a narrow channel of water and a small portion of beach separated her from her companions.

Gracefully she breasted the water and crossed over. At the channel's edge she paused, momentarily worn out by her long endeavour. She then covered the remaining yards. Despite the devouring pain, joy surged within her. On reaching her friends she gave a muffled cackle of greeting and contentment. But the silent flock promptly rose and flew away, leaving the stricken one to the engulfing darkness.

The Dig Out

On a crystalline morning a friend John and I set out for a day's fishing, deep in the Ecuadorian Andes. The fishing place in question, the Rio Chalupas, was so remote that we even fancied our chances of making one of the rarest of sightings – a fabled spectacled bear. We talked of the possibility as we drove along past shapely, snow-capped Cotopaxi and on through earthen laneways, flanked by blue-green eucalyptus. Eventually we found ourselves out on the endless paramos with their tufted *ichu* grass and tall *frailejones*, so called because, especially when shrouded in Andean mists, these plants resembled cowled grey friars.

It would take four hours driving across the paramos to reach our fishing spot. We had left early, though, and we knew that on reaching our destination the fishing would be good. The very inaccessibility of the place ensured that it was by no means overfished. The boisterous mountain stream simply teemed with trout; catching a hundred in a day was a distinct possibility.

The earthen road we followed between the mountains snaked interminably through the paramos. As we drew nearer to our destination, it began to deteriorate. Although we were in the dry summer season, there obviously had been some unexpected rains in this particular area, because sections were quite muddy and hard to negotiate. But John was an excellent driver and seemed to be coping quite well.

I worried about the reliability of our vehicle in such deteriorating terrain. It was a type of utility jeep used by Germans in World War II: canvas roof, metal body and, ominously, only two-wheel drive – back wheels. Fishermen usually only ventured into these parts in four-wheel drive jeeps and generally they had two vehicles – one to haul the other out in case it got irrevocably embedded in mud.

We were distracted by a heartening sight: it was the sun dancing on the Rio Chalupas way below us. But our joy had barely reg-

THE DIG OUT

istered when our jeep sank to the front axle in mud. John made valiant attempts to extricate it. The engine roared, the wheels spun, but there was no movement. If anything, once he took his foot off the accelerator, it subsided more profoundly into the slime. What to do? We had no way of getting out of this morass.

Very much on our minds were some friends of ours who found themselves in this exact situation some months before. Their position was somewhat better because they had a robust four-wheel-drive jeep. Nevertheless, try as they might, they could not get the vehicle to move. Eventually they decided that the only solution was to trek back to civilisation. There were four of them and it meant a long march through the mountains on a bitter Andean night. It was agonising. They had to try and keep together, which wasn't easy, for one of them had flat feet and the soles of those feet became massive blisters. No thought could be given to sitting down for even a brief respite. To do so could easily result in falling asleep and dying of hypothermia. One of the party, peering through the darkness, thought he detected something moving. He had a small torch in his pocket which he shone where he thought he had detected the movement. There was a wolf, circling, waiting for him to falter. After a ten-hour odyssey, they reached a tarmac road and caught a bus back to Quito. They stretched out in the aisle between the seats of the bus and never opened an eye till they were vigorously roused from sleep in Quito.

Their story now haunted us. John and I looked at each other hopelessly. Then, prompted I don't know by what, I said to my companion: 'John, you stay here with the jeep and I'll go and see what I can find.' What I expected to find on these harsh uplands that stretched like the wastes of Antarctica in all directions I don't know. Indeed I thought of Captain Oates walking out of the tent in a blizzard so that his companions might have a better chance of survival on Scott's ill-fated expedition to the South Pole. And I recalled those immortal words: 'I am just going outside and may be some time.' Brave man, but the difference between him and myself was that he knew exactly what he was doing and why.

First I walked down to the Rio Chalupas. There was a grassy knoll by the stream studded with white margaritas, lupins and gentians. With compassion I noted the extremely short stems of these flowers; they hugged the ground so as to survive the fierce winds that frequently funnelled and lamented through the mountains on these elevated plateaus. The place wasn't called Huairemontes for nothing. I had been here before. To my left I could see the conical arctic beauty of Huairemonte. One luminous night I saw it palely lit by a full moon. It was freezing and later, as I lay huddled in my tent awaiting sleep, a herd of wild horses galloped by outside, as though having taken fright at something. Unforgettable moments.

I continued my aimless walk, instinctively feeling somehow I should do so. As I moved through the *ichu* grass, I could feel it grating against my trousers. I kept on through the vast sameness. I looked to the distant place where they say the almost mythical spectacled bear was once spotted. Nothing stirring there today. Then, a slight mound barely caught my attention in this wasteland. On closer inspection, it proved to be a type of bivouac composed of sods. Peering into its dark cavern I descried – to my astonishment – a pickaxe, mattock and spade! I was afraid to take my eyes off them lest they should disappear. It was tantamount to stumbling upon a deep well of icy water while dying of thirst amid the immense burning sands of the Sahara.

John's eyes grew saucer-like with wonder and disbelief as I returned laden with these tools.

'Where on earth did you get those in this place?'
'Just out there.'
'JUST OUT THERE!'
'Yes, I simply came across them. It was a bit of luck.'
'That has to be the understatement of the century. By comparison this makes the chance of winning the lottery fade into insignificance.'

Much relieved he began to dig vigorously and I joined him. We cleared the mud and clay from around the jeep, put *ichu* and twigs under the wheels in an effort to give them some traction. Then John started the engine, put the vehicle into reverse and backed out of the hole, not without much skidding, from which I got a muddy face. Having by now lost any stomach for fishing through frayed nerves, we gratefully headed for home without delay. John had to deal with a few more dubious surfaces. We held our breath. At last he got on to firmer ground. As I said, he was an excellent driver.

The strange thing about this story is that it is absolutely true.

A Curious Sighting

It was a rare morning, even for Quito, as I set out with about thirty of my standard four primary school pupils for a day's outing in the Andes. The sun glittered in a sky of such a delicate blue that it was almost invisible, giving the impression that one was situated nowhere. Such was not the case, of course, we were headed in a truck for a *hacienda* that nestled among the mountains, a *hacienda* that had a fine swimming pool.

On arrival, the boys lost no time in diving into the pool, not without gasps of pain. Although Ecuador, as its name suggests, is situated on the equator, it is an elevated country and its capital, Quito, sits at 9252 feet above sea level. This causes the night temperatures to fall considerably, because the atmosphere is heated by the intense sun and once it disappears the thermometer plummets. So, even on this gracious morning, the water in the pool was bracing. Once in, however, the boys swam, dived, splashed and wallowed about with abandon. I stood by with my whistle, making sure that things didn't get too robust.

When the lads had utterly exhausted themselves, they came out of the pool, opened their knapsacks, took out sandwiches, bananas – great restorers of energy – colas and began to picnic. Liberated from school, they chattered like a flock of starlings assembling to migrate.

Eventually, the chatter ceased and they commenced to lie about on the surrounding grass, resting and absorbing some cheering sun. As mentioned, they had exhausted themselves in the pool and, besides, the journey in the truck – which the boys dubbed the *trucutu*, after the police vehicle used for riot control – had been rocky. Truth to tell, I was tired myself and was glad to lie down and gaze dreamily into the profundities of space. At the very zenith of the sky there were wispy white clouds – destined to figure significantly in this story.

Little by little I began to let my eyes wander over the trackless

A CURIOUS SIGHTING

skies. And then I spotted it, little more than a speck on the edge of the horizon to my left. As it approached it grew in size and materialised into a silvery, saucer-like craft – indeed the description 'flying saucer' would have fitted it to perfection. Some of the boys had also begun to see it. And one of them cried out, 'Look! Sputnik!' Another added, 'Laika is lookin out the window, searching for a tree.' Boys! Even at the most solemn moments. Why Laika, the Soviet space dog, would be looking for a tree is another matter, since the animal was in fact a bitch.

Yet the year was 1958 and the Sputnik era. This could indeed be Sputnik. It speedily approached until it was directly above our heads in the neighbourhood of those ever so distant wispy clouds. At that point it stopped. No, it was not Sputnik. Satellites don't stop. They continue along an orbital path. So, whatever this craft was, it was no satellite.

What was it, we wondered. Were there creatures within closely observing us as we stood there? There was an undoubted whiff of menace. All had now got to their feet. The craft must have been radiating heat or some chemical, because the wispy clouds summarily disappeared.

As we stood mesmerised, it hovered way up there for some fifteen minutes. Then it veered sharply at right angles and within seconds was situated on the remote horizon to our backs. Further proof that this was not a satellite – they don't veer off at right angles from their orbiting path.

The UFO, for such it was, hovered in its new position again for some fifteen minutes. Then, in a matter of seconds, it shot gleaming in the clear day to the opposite horizon and vanished from sight. The whole episode had lasted for thirty minutes plus.

Fifty years later I still have no way of explaining what exactly this object was or where it came from. The 'saucer' didn't land, nor did any little green men disembark. Were beings from some faraway galaxy curious about the 'signs in the heavens' caused by the Sputnik phenomenon? Or about the satellite tracking station the US had built in the region? I don't know, nor do I wish to make any such claims. I simply describe what I and the pupils saw. Was it just imagination? Or mass hallucination? Possibly, but again I feel no necessity to argue regarding these matters. I might observe, though, that the mystery has an ancient pedigree, for Virgil (70-19 BCE) makes a reference to *disci volantes* – flying saucers – in his classic poem the *Aeneid*. Yes, even that long ago!

Death, Where Is Thy Sting? I

Fr Ortiz was as dead as a bludgened seal. Died of heart failure on the operation table. His family, who lived in a city some four hours away, had been informed and were on their way to the obsequies. His Salesian brothers were anticipating the arrival of his remains at the chapel of Don Bosco College.

Meanwhile the body lay still on the operating table.

Soon afterwards the surgeon who performed the operation was passing through the theatre. He gave a brief glance at the body – and froze. He was sure that they had left the corpse prone on its back. How did it come to be tilted slightly to one side? Checking the body, he thought he detected faint stirrings of life; so faint that he couldn't even be sure of their existence. Nevertheless he decided to raise the alarm and speedily reassembled the surgical team.

The surgeon barked peremptory orders. And the bustling group urgently administered oxygen, massage, electric shocks … The intensity of the shocks caused the body to leap upwards from the table. The team worked arduously. Perspiration commenced to glisten on their foreheads. Then, at last (!), there were slight flutterings on the heart monitor. Slowly the heart resumed its beat to a loud gasp of surprise and relief from the team. Fr Ortiz had risen from the dead.

One year later, I was taking him on a drive through a panoramic Andean valley on a blue day so glorious, it appeared unreal. We stopped to take it all in. A scarlet cardinal perched on a tree near us. Fr Ortiz grew pensive. Then, unexpectedly, he said: 'If the good Lord left me here, it must have been for some purpose. I hope I can fulfil it.' He lived on for five good years. I wonder did he fulfil his purpose? I do know that he became a loving and much loved man. Maybe that was what it was about.

Death, Where Is Thy Sting? II

(I here intrude the tale of Brother Vicky in the section on 'Latin American Days', because it touches on the same theme as the foregoing story, though it took place elsewhere.)

Brother Vicky was born in Cape Town early in the twentieth century. His parents were circus folk and were performing in the city at the time of his birth.

When the troupe left Cape Town, Vicky was still a baby and for some reason his parents entrusted him to the orphanage run by the Sisters of Nazareth. They may have had the intention of returning to fetch him later. They never did. Maybe they got lost in the wars of those days. You would think that, as a result, Vicky would have become a morose child. Not at all. He was surely one of the most cheerful people that ever lived.

When he completed his time at the orphanage, he went into care at the Salesian Institute and was so enamoured of the place that, once his education was complete, he happily joined the Salesian order.

He spent his long life as a Salesian. The Salesians, following in the footsteps of their founder, Don Bosco, were totally devoted to the welfare of youth, especially the poorest of them. And Vicky had a real talent for this work. Just to meet this bubbly little man with the laughing eyes was in itself a tonic, for he was a born entertainer. People said it was in his blood, having come from circus folk. All his life he could charm children with his jokes, magic tricks and multiple shenanigans.

Not only did he captivate the children but also he managed the more demanding task of impressing his Salesian brothers. His party piece on Christmas Day was to sing 'The Rose of Tralee'. He would appear immaculately dressed in tailed coat, dickybow and shiny top hat. As he sang the first line of the song 'The pale moon was rising above the green mountain', he would dramatically remove his top hat to reveal a pale-moonish, bald pate to all present! He really could use his assets.

But the real point of this tale is to tell of Brother Vicky's life-threatening operation. There was a strong possibility that, at his age, he wouldn't survive it. So, while he was being rolled up to the theatre, there were many Salesian brothers and friends there to wish him well. A good number could scarcely keep the tears from their eyes. Unable to resist the availability of an audience, however, the ever cheerful Vicky rose to the occasion and, as he was being wheeled in, started waving to the onlookers and sang: 'Wish me luck as you wave me goodbye / Cheerio, here I go on my way.' An entertainer to the last.

Vicky, of course, was not without critics. Who is? One solemn friend of his said: 'The problem with Vicky is that he never grew up!' But wasn't it the Man himself who said: 'Unless you become like little children ...' Thank God Brother Vicky never grew up.

Death, Where Is Thy Sting? III

(The following story doesn't belong to 'American Days' either, but I believe it has to go here because of an important point it makes.)

Fr Tommy, an old African missionary, lay dying. A number of his companions hastily gathered at his bedside. Holding lighted candles, they were reciting prayers for the dying, while Tommy lay on his bed, comatose. The solemn words of the litany echoed round the death chamber:

Saint Francis and Saint Dominic	pray for him
Saint Francis Xavier	pray for him
St John Vianney	pray for him
Saint Catherine	pray for him
Saint Teresa	pray for him
St Thomas	pray for him
All holy men and women	pray for him

Suddenly, Tommy's eyes opened. To everyone's amazement, he sat up and looked at them in open-mouthed wonder. Then, having grasped what was happening, with a little mischievous look, he simply said, 'Sorry, lads, flight delayed.'

Angry Fish

'One missing!' Sisters Margaret and Sheila informed us with alarm. They had just counted the group of boys following a swim in the Pacific. We had a group of shoeshine boys from Quito on a week's holiday by the coast, accompanied by the two sisters, David – a volunteer – and myself. Where was the missing one? We looked speedily towards the minor cliff of white sand to our backs. He might be sitting at its base. A snake was crawling up its surface. This would have been a source of fear and excitement, if we didn't have enough cause for fear and excitement already. All of us then turned our eyes to the glittering surface of the sea. Far out someone descried something floating. Could be the missing youth, some felt. While discussing this briefly with the sisters, I took my gaze off the waters. When I turned to them again, David had already started swimming strongly towards the distant object.

Almost immediately an old fisherman appeared on the scene. He was barefoot, with tight-fitting pants, wide-brimmed straw hat and weather-beaten whipcord body. He looked your quintessential old man of the sea. With eyes narrowed in his wrinkled face, he scanned the ocean. Then looked at the swimming David and whined in alarm: *Pesce bravo!* He had spotted the 'angry fish' – a shark. Now, instead of losing one, we were going to lose two. I also shouted a warning after David, but all to no avail. His urgent, strenuous swimming seemed to cut out both the old man's voice and my own.

There was nothing we could do but stand by helplessly and hope. Even in the Pacific sun, my face whitened and my knees faltered as David swam towards the floating object and the area in which the 'angry fish' supposedly was. The agony of all of us was drawn out as the brave swimmer inched towards his goal – and what else? The mind boggled.

One of the bigger boys offered to follow David and was already moving towards the sea. Haunted by visions of greater bloodshed, I quickly discouraged him from doing so.

The agony of all went on, and on. The old man, prophet of doom, had disappeared as mysteriously as he appeared.

After what seemed an eternity, David reached the floating object, clung to it for some minutes and then started the long journey back. He had obviously been resting on it.

If the journey outward was tense, it was nothing compared with the return. We knew that every stroke took him nearer to safety, but the terror that he might not do so increased. It was nail-biting. What was he to the shark, after all, if not a tempting piece of bait bobbing about in an endless sea? If that mighty creature gave chase, there would be no contest. Sharks can swim at up to 40 kilometres per hour. They do not see so well, but are unerringly guided by vibrations. Even if David knew of the presence of the menacing creature – which he didn't – floating motionless on the water, waiting for it to go away, might not be an option. There was no reason to suppose that it was going anywhere and there was the distinct possibility that it would be joined by others.

Sharks, in fact, don't eat frequently and David's best hope was that the one in his vicinity, and quite aware of his presence, had recently eaten and was not hungry. Unlike humans, they do not kill wantonly. So I have been told.

Nevertheless, it was with the deepest anxiety that we all watched the bobbing head of our friend as little by little he approached the shore. Each one of us was like a fisherman, intently watching his lure yet, quite unlike him, the last thing we wanted to see was that lure suddenly dragged down beneath the surface.

At last, to everyone's great relief, David staggered on to the beach and sank exhausted to the sand as, bewildered, he got a hero's welcome. No one told him of the drama he had been engaged in. At that moment, because of his depleted state, he probably could not have handled it. The story could wait until later.

No one who was there on that day has ever forgotten those happenings. David survived, of course, but they were spared none of the feelings and anxieties that went with the drama. It brought all face to face with their own mortality and forever left a scar on their psyche.

As for the 'missing boy', he actually appeared shortly after

David had launched out into the deep to recover what possibly could have been his body. He had wandered off unnoticed behind a sandhill to have a pee! Yes, it was bathetic. The 'body' out at sea was only a floating log. It, at least, did offer David the possibility of the rest that brought him safely back to his mightily relieved friends.

Home Thoughts from Abroad

A lone Irishman, far from home, I was staying in a provincial town on the verge of the Ecuadorian jungle. I was beginning to learn Spanish and struggled to communicate with those around me, which exacerbated my isolation. I myself knew from experience that there is nothing as frustrating as trying to hold a conversation with someone who is racking the files of his mind looking for the word he needs. People were kind and, from the interesting depths of their conversations, would occasionally toss a few words in my direction, so that I wouldn't feel left out. And then quickly return to their topic. If the reader has experienced this phenomenon, you will know that in this situation you feel as helpless as a baby.

The building in which I was staying had an inner courtyard ringed by a resounding wooden corridor where you could walk while being protected from either fierce tropical sun or ravaging tropical downpour. I was strolling on this corridor one afternoon, when I was approached shyly by an Italian, Antonio Bellini, whom I knew slightly.

'When I was a boy in Italy during the First World War,' he told me, 'there were some English soldiers stationed in our town who used to sing some nice songs.'

'Can you remember the songs?'

'Look, I didn't have a word of English then, and I don't have a word of English now, so I understood nothing of what they were singing.'

'What a pity.'

'Oh, I remember the tunes and all the words. It's just that I have no idea what the words mean.'

'Could you sing one of them for me?'

'I don't have much of a voice,' he said, as he cleared his throat like a 'reluctant' singer in an Irish pub and, then, in perfect English gave a sonorous rendering of:

'It's a long way to Tipperary,
It's a long way to go…'

And then:

'Oh, oh Antonio has gone away,
Left me all alone-io…'

In that place, under the searing sun, with jungle macaws calling raucously in the background, this lonely Irishman's eyes got misty.

* * *

On the same trip, I entered a town called Porto Viejo. This was fifty years ago. I'm sure it looks totally different now, but in those days it was strongly reminiscent of the frontier towns you saw in the Hollywood movies. Dirt roads and horses tied outside grubby saloons.

Again I was the lone Irishman far from home. And into the bargain, young and inexperienced. But as I strolled about, I got a huge surprise. I was confronted by a shop that bore the name McBride! I was afraid to take my eyes off it lest it disappear. The contents of the shop were indeed varied: boiled sweets in jars, shoe polish, fruit and vegetables, saddle for a horse, a bridle – yes, 'hanging on the wall' – and so forth. And there behind the counter with dark hair but blue eyes and fair skin stood, I supposed, Mr McBride. I addressed him in English. 'Are you from Ireland, Mr McBride?'

He looked at me uncomprehendingly, and then corrected my pronunciation. His name was pronounced 'Macbreeday', he told me in Spanish, adding, 'No speak English.'

'But your name, McBride, is Irish,' I said, struggling with my Spanish. 'Where did your ancestors come from?'

He had a vague family memory that they came from somewhere far over the sea, but could not say where exactly they came from, or when.

I supposed myself that some forebear of his may have come as a mercenary to join the ranks of Simon Bolivar in the War of Independence. Many did. I found a street in Quito, capital of Ecuador, called 'General O'Leary' for an Irishman who fought with Bolivar and Sucre in the liberation of Ecuador. Yet, there now stood Mr McBride, with Celtic blood flowing in his veins like myself, who had become more Ecuadorean than the Ecuadoreans themselves. He had no sense of affinity with me, no glint of empathy in his eye. So I bought some boiled sweets and went out on to the dirt road with an aching heart.

Not Our World

I slipped into San Camilo's Hospital to see my friend Teresa. She was pregnant and hospitalised for some minor matter connected with the pregnancy. With me I brought some food and medicine, both of which were in short supply.

On entering the rundown hospital, my nostrils were assailed not by the antiseptic smells one usually associates with hospitals, but rather by acrid human odours emanating from grubby wards.

I walked into Ward 8 and made towards Teresa's bed. It was empty. I turned to the surrounding patients. They were staring at me in silence.

'Teresa?'

'Didn't you know?' asked one woman.

'Know what?'

'Teresa died last night.'

'Died!' I was dumbfounded. 'She wasn't even seriously ill.'

They looked at me, pity and fear blending in their dark eyes, and I wished I hadn't said what I had just said.

'Where is she?'

'In the morgue.'

Leaving the food and medicine to Teresa's most immediate neighbours, I walked towards the morgue as though in a trance.

There she lay on a cold slab in her well-worn poncho. Lying there too were a couple of dead babies with ancient grimacing faces, their bodies shrivelled and blue. Teresa's face, lined yet beautiful, looked at rest. The unequal struggle for survival was over.

I lingered there, pondering her toilsome life. Images and memories crowded my mind. One of my tenderest recollections was of finding her once trying to sell some folkloric dolls of her own making on a busy sidewalk. She shrank into a corner, mute and unobtrusive, while displaying the merchandise on outstretched hands. A sensitive and shy person, poor yet proud, it could not have been at all easy for her. Only the desperation of having hungry little mouths at home could have forced her into this one entrepreneurial adventure.

Then there was the evening of the awesome landslide that crushed the lives out of twenty of her neighbours. A municipal engineer, constructing a road for the convenience of tourists further up the mountain, criminally allowed earth to pile up and up until torrential rain forced the slimy monster down to overwhelm the hovels of the poor beneath. Those who lost their lives were mostly children, engulfed in an instant as they sat doing homework or knelt by primus stoves cooking something for their parents, who would soon arrive home, shattered by having carried crushing burdens on their backs all the livelong day around the market on the Avenida 6 de Diciembre.

Only the previous Sunday some of these children had made their First Holy Communion. Teresa had prepared them over long months. Now all that would remain of the occasion for the bereaved would be the smiling faces frozen forever in black-and-white photographs. These would be treasured for years and years to come until finally overtaken by creeping oblivion and dimmed by smoke and time.

There, in the front row of one such photograph, stood little Elena, who was found clasping her baby brother to her breast. Her demented parents returned to find five of their seven children wiped out. Five. The father died soon afterwards. They say he was drunk and fell from a building. Maybe.

How Teresa plied the men with steaming *canilla* through that long and tortured night as they extracted bodies, some dead, some still living, from the amorphous mass of slime. How defeated she looked as Lucco Mendez was discovered crouching intact on a chair in an alcove. He had died as the air ran out. That was the spot where Teresa urged the men to dig immediately following the accident but, unfortunately, she was overruled by the boy's father, who felt that he must be elsewhere.

And how her eyes smouldered with silent indignation as the municipal engineer haggled with Señor Mendez about compensation for his home and his son. 'State a sum,' said the official with pencil poised.

'I don't want to ask too much,' said Mendez meekly.

'Indeed I know that. Nevertheless, state a sum. Not too much, as you say.'

In the immediate aftermath of the tragedy, Teresa threw open the door of her humble abode to the homeless.

No less heroic than the occasion of the landslide – for me at least – were all those other arduous days which Teresa spent washing other people's laundry for a mere pittance in the local *lavanderia*. Indeed having given birth once, next day found her at her post with the newborn baby fastened securely to her back. One could only marvel at the physical toughness and inner strength of the woman. And she was always ready with a smile and a greeting as she scrubbed and scrubbed on stones worn away by years of persistent love.

Recovering from my reverie, I slowly left the hospital. On the way out I passed the staff-room and bitterly heard the talk and laughter of those sipping coffee within.

The family remonstrated with the doctors about Teresa's death, but in the plaintive, abject manner of the downtrodden who perceive their rights as favours. Predictably, the medics dismissed them, not just brusquely, but even with scorn. How dare the *cholos*!

'May the angels lead you into paradise; may the martyrs come to welcome you and take you to the holy city ... Where Lazarus is poor no longer, may you have eternal rest,' prayed Teresa's good friend, Padre Juan, as she was being taken out for burial. The grave was filled in, the earth falling upon the coffin with thudding finality and the green sward was placed on top.

Sixteen-year-old Pedro, Teresa's son, stood quietly weeping beside his father, Tomas. Suddenly he threw himself upon the grave and burst into loud sobs as he beat the earth with futile fists: 'My mother went into hospital healthy and sound,' he wailed. 'Those doctors killed her. Assassins!' Without knowing it, the lad had a point. A nurse had come to the ward and called out 'Señora Teresa!' His mother identified herself and was given an injection. Unfortunately, a recently admitted woman was also Teresa, but said nothing – with fatal consequences.

All the mourners looked on with stoic and hopeless faces.
Tomas raised up his son. 'Hush now, Pedrito.' And he comforted him.
'Papi, this is not our world,' wept Pedro.
'There's nothing to do, son.'
But Pedro's encircling hands clenched upon his father's back.

A Lesson in Love

I closed the youth centre in La Colmena and bade my young friends goodnight. I then drove precipitously down the cobblestone streets and found my way round to the Via Oriental by way of Villa Flora and Colegio Montufar. To my left there was a dark chasm where the Rio Machangara slashed a deep wound in the fertile land – the work of millennia. The boisterous river, angrily foaming and lashing at the rocks below, was only a distant sigh from the newly constructed Via Oriental.

On rounding a bend in the road, I was confronted by someone lying in the path of my jeep. Braking hard, I stopped with a screech and a jolt. Only inches separated us. A quick check to the rear for oncoming headlights revealed that no car was in sight, so I backed, drew into the side, leaving my hazard lights flashing.

I approached the prone figure (a dog lay beside it) without apprehension at first, but then cautiously. Was it a set-up? Actually there was no need to worry; it was an Indian in a drunken stupor. The dog growled. I made a little run at the beast. He scurried away. No need to bother about him; he was a coward. I shook the Indian. The only response was a loud snore. I shook him again vigorously. This time there were mutterings and grumblings in a thick voice.

I hauled him out of harm's way. God, but he was dead weight! Once I got him to the grass margin, I rested. Wisps of breath ascended into the sharp night air. My headlights lit up the broad, bronzed face of the Indian with its high cheekbones and slowed eyes. The healed scars on that countenance told of a despairing life of drunken brawls and brutalisation. A pastor who was once trying to wean such a man from his drinking habits was told, 'Drink and sex are my only joys in life, padre.'

I couldn't leave him there by the roadside. He might stumble under one of those great articulated lorries that plied between the uplands and the coast and could not be as readily halted as a jeep.

Nearby there was a grassy knoll. Feeling that he would be safe if I got him to the far side of it, I began to drag him over with the utmost difficulty. More mutterings and grumblings and certainly no co-operation. Just then I was bitten on the ankle by the slinking dog, who promptly took to his heels. I finally edged my burden under a ledge that had been cut out of the mountainside to make way for the new road. Gently I covered him with his stout red poncho, feeling as elated as a boy scout who has done his good deed for the day.

It was then that the man momentarily opened his eyes and growled, 'Son of a bitch! You can't even let a poor so-and-so get a few winks of sleep.'

Feeling ill-used, I arose and with open arms appealed to the long-suffering Andes. They just stood bemused and noncommittal. I looked to the stars. They winked impishly back at me from the patient infinity of space. Eventually I sank on my haunches and rocked with silent laughter. And that ankle was still giving me hell which meant that I would have to get shots against rabies. Not a pleasant prospect, but you couldn't take chances.

Candy for the Kids

A full, burnished moon lurked somewhere in the heavens, but was obscured by 'moistery' clouds, as the procession set out with a few young people at its head bearing a huge cross covered with multicoloured and intricate psychedelic patterns. The scene was lit by a flaming torch that momentarily summoned faces out of the dark and wanly lit the moistened cobblestone street. All was silence except for the shuffling of feet.

The crowd halted and gathered round the now upright cross. 'First station,' announced a young man, 'Jesus is condemned to death by Pilate.' He continued. 'It is now nearly two thousand years since Jesus, the innocent one, was shamefully condemned to death by Pilate. That's a long time ago. What has all that got to do with us now, you may ask? Well, remember the little boy Diego Chavez whose strange blue eyes (most of our eyes are dark) and mischievous smile gave joy to our *barrio*. It is barely two months since he died of typhoid, because the water from our wells is dirty and the authorities just don't care. We poor are expendable. Somewhere, a Pilate washed his hands of responsibility and condemned little Diego to die. The passion of Jesus continues. He was condemned anew in that child. "Truly, I say to you, as you did it to one of the least of these, you did it to me ..." With the help of Christ, the Liberator, may we find the strength to stand up in love and say *No* to the tyranny that does such awful things to us.'

'Amen,' chorused the gathering. And a woman's voice led them in reciting the Pater, Ave, and Gloria. They then went on with their way of the cross.

***

'Second station,' said a woman, 'the cross is laid on the shoulder of Jesus ... All of us have been to the market on the Avenida America, and we have seen the terrible loads that are put on the back of our fellow countryman, the Indian, who is used like a beast of burden.

The sight has always filled me with indignation and moved me to tears. As a young girl, I remember seeing an unfortunate man struggling up our street with a cruel burden. A leather band was round his forehead like a halter and, as he strained beneath the load, sweat streamed down his poor face. I wiped it with a cloth and began to help him with his burden. It seemed the natural thing to do. But a woman following on behind cried out with a harsh voice, "Get out of the way, you little busybody, and mind your own affairs. This *indio* is being well paid for his work." Well paid! One peso. The man turned his deep eyes upon me and gasped, "*Gracias niñita.*" Something in the depths of those eyes left me standing there, sorrowful, yet awed and profoundly at peace. My sisters and brothers, the cross is laid on the shoulders of Jesus every day in the Avenida America.'

***

'Fourth station – Jesus meets his most afflicted mother,' said a young mother with a baby asleep in her arms. 'What a sad meeting for Mary as she sees her only son dragged away to be crucified. But like Antonio remarked at the first station, these are not just things that happened long ago. Here among us we have Maria Teresa. One evening on this very street, returning from her long day's work at the market, she met her son, Roberto, as he was being dragged away by security police because he led a student protest at the raising of bus fares. We poor know only too well that when bus fares go up, everything goes up. That was five years ago. There has not been trace or tiding of him since. Maria Teresa has worn out her shoes looking for news of him in every prison, in every barracks. All in vain. She went to a prelate and asked him to approach the government. He said to her, "Imagine that your son was taken up in an aeroplane and dropped into the sea. He's gone. Forget about him." Forget about him! As if a mother could ever do that. Jesus would never have given such an answer. Our country, and all of Latin America, is full of sorrowing Marys who have seen their sons and daughters dragged away and disappear without trace. Let us pray for Roberto. Let us pray for Maria Teresa. Like her, we must have the courage to go on wearing out our shoes and raising the voice of protest till justice is done. Our Father who art in heaven ...'

***

'Eighth station, the women of Jerusalem weep over Jesus,' intoned a woman of African origin with headscarf and frank, open face – serious, patient and long-suffering. She too had a baby in her arms that sucked upon its soother. 'At this moment of awful suffering,' she continued, 'the thoughts of Jesus were not for himself, but for the tragedy that would befall these women. Jerusalem was soon to be besieged by the Romans and the women and children of that city would starve. In war it's always the women and children that suffer most. And today it's the women and children that still suffer most. I myself am oppressed three times over. I'm oppressed because I am poor; I'm oppressed because I am a woman; and I'm oppressed because I am black. My brothers and sisters, before confronting the mighty who grind us to dust, we ourselves must stop walking on one another.'

A look of uneasy self-discovery crept over many a face.

At this point, a police car appeared on the scene and started to prowl behind the crowd as it moved from station to station. Within the vehicle were three local officers and a gringo secret agent. On a tip from an informer and on behalf of the military dictatorship they were checking out this gathering, including its priest, for communist subversives.

***

'Tenth station - Jesus is stripped of his garments ...'

'Note well the face of that young brat speaking, sergeant,' said Capitán Anaya, one of the four, who sat in the front of the police car and, even at night, took refuge behind dark glasses.

'*Si, mi capitán,*' replied Sergeant Gomez, the driver.

'And search out the others who seem to be marshalling this demonstration.'

'*Si, mi capitán.*'

'Can you point out that priest – your friend and fellow gringo who works in this godforsaken hole, Señor Woods?' Anaya asked the secret agent who was in the back of the car.

'Yes, the one towards the rear with the polo-neck sweater. That is he.' And he pointed out the priest with his forefinger.

'Polo-neck sweater,' said Anaya with disdain. 'God be with the old soutane. Those were real priests, who kept people's thoughts focused on eternity. Somehow you could control priests in soutanes. Not so these subversives in polo-neck sweaters. We must stamp out these communists.'

'Maybe we should just pick him up straightaway and be done with it,' said Gomez.

'Easy, sergeant,' intervened Anaya. 'Remember the eighth point of the Plan our gringo friends gave us.'

'*Si, mi capitán,*' Gomez replied, and went on in a robot-like monotone: 'Arrests should be made in the countryside, on deserted streets or late at night. Once a priest has been arrested, the Minister should plant subversive material in his briefcase and, if possible, in his room or home, and a weapon, preferably a high calibre pistol. Have a story prepared disgracing him before his bishop and the public.'

'But Sergeant Gomez is much more interested in point eleven: Reward the agents who best work at enforcing this plan-of-action by giving them the belongings confiscated from the homes of priests and religious.' This was muttered in a thick voice by an *agente* seated beside Woods.

'Pay no attention to Agente Henriquez, Señor Woods,' suggested Anaya. 'He's boozed. Overdid it at that pub we were checking out earlier.'

'Look out at this impoverished *barrio*, Meester Woods,' continued Henriquez. 'A Gulag created by you *yanquis*.'

'*Agente!*' interposed Anaya sharply.

'What about the inalienable right to life, liberty and the pursuit of happiness, Meester Woods? Not for export?' the intoxicated officer persisted.

'That's quite enough. I'm warning you, *agente*.' Anaya once again sternly reprimanded the fractious Henriquez. 'Don't mind him, Señor Woods. When sober, he's our most effective operative.'

'*In vino veritas,*' remarked Woods coldly. He'd been a seminarist in his day.

'Why can't America be the champion of freedom it's supposed to be?'

'Enough, I said!'

CANDY FOR THE KIDS

Henriquez lapsed into a sullen and drowsed silence...

The procession was in motion again. Suddenly, an Indian, bare from the waist up, staggered in from the darkness and insisted on helping to carry the cross. He too was intoxicated.

'This is going to make a farce out of the whole thing,' exulted Anaya.

The organisers also expected spoiling laughter. The Indian staggered along with the cross and, falling theatrically under its weight, lay spread-eagled there on the ground. Nobody laughed. But many an eye was moist with tears.

The police car impatiently blurped a brief warning. The people separated and it sped through the crowd, its blue revolving light slashing the faces of the onlookers.

***

'Twelfth station – Jesus dies on the cross.' A teenage girl was speaking. 'We see Jesus die at the hands of the powerful ones of the world. The Roman soldiers drew lots for his garments, just as unspeakable men drew lots for the pleasure of murdering our own Saint Romero at the altar. But Jesus rose from the dead and lives forever, and Saint Romero too lives forever in our hearts and in the new courage we feel in facing oppression...'

***

'Sergeant,' said Anaya, 'would you make a stop at Herrera's little corner shop. They usually stay open quite late and I daren't go home without getting some candy for the kids.'

'*Si, mi capitán.*'

African Days

God Is a Catholic

The weary travellers descended the steps of the UTA plane and were submerged in the hot humid night. A number of ladies were already there on the tarmac beaming a toothy greeting – their mission was obvious enough. Within the dimly lit airport the motley group of passengers made their way to a desk marked 'passports'. A solitary fan whirred uselessly overhead, as perspiration coursed down the faces of all. To one side a sizeable heap of dun butterflies awaited the dustpan.

As I approached the desk, I noticed the khaki-clad official ask a tall, Out-of-Africa, flaxen-haired man to step aside. When my turn came, the sprightly police inspector, for such he was, flicked through my passport.

'There's no visa here.'

'That's right.'

'Why not?'

'I'm only a transit passenger and will be leaving here in six hours. I was told at the French Embassy in Lusaka, which takes care of your business there, that I didn't need a visa.'

'Well, you do.'

'Sorry about that, but that's what they told me.'

'Just stand aside.'

The exchange had been without rancour.

Soon afterwards a glowing, curly-haired Italian approached the official brandishing a passport.

'You don't have a visa.' He was in exactly in the same position as the flaxen-haired fellow and myself.

'You see, I will go early in the morning. I do not need the visa.'

'You cannot enter without one.'

'What you mean no can enter? I am the transit pass – *passeggero*. I don't need the visa,' the Italian's voice was becoming querulous and his hands were beginning to gesticulate.

'But why do you argue? I've already explained to you that you need a visa.'

'You explain me nothing. I repeat, I am only the transit *passeggero*. Visa! Visa!' he exploded. 'Who you think you are anyway? The United States of America? Little half-assed country!' His arms were going like windmills.

It was the sort of animated exchange you might hear a thousand times in Italy. Unaware of this, many of the onlookers were startled and open-mouthed.

'Stand aside, please,' said the quietly smouldering inspector to his new adversary.

When all the passports had been duly processed, the inspector approached the three of us who had been detained. He took the Dutch passport of the flaxen-haired man and my own, but pointedly ignored the glowering Italian. He perused our documents at length and seemed to be awaiting an initiative on our part. There was probably no difficulty here that a few dollars couldn't solve. Anyone but a neophyte in Africa would have realised that. Yet, rightly or wrongly, I had a principle and I don't know what the Dutchman had – the same perhaps or an acute shortage of money – but neither of us bit.

After a long and pregnant pause, the inspector brought us to a locked and barred room. He unlocked the door. The room was full of luggage. We were asked to identify our baggage, which was set aside, and the room was then relocked.

We were led into a dingy office lit by a solitary low-watt bulb hanging naked from the ceiling. A police sergeant, who had been resting his head on a desk, roused himself as we entered and donned a box-like French police cap. The inspector handed him the three passports and spoke with him in the local language. The sergeant glanced at the Italian and the inspector left.

The sergeant sleepily investigated the passports. I saw him looking at mine which, for a moment, he held upside-down. He too examined the documents for what seemed an age.

'You want your passports back?'

'Of course.'

He went on with his perusing, occasionally looking at us quizzically. The game was continuing.

At last our apparent crassness caused him to give up. 'You must surrender your hand luggage,' he demanded. Now my cash was in a money-belt round my body, but everything in my pilot's bag was essential for the work I did; I refused point-blank to part with it. There was a tug of war between the sergeant and myself. To my surprise he gave way. There was something considerate about that face.

Virtually quarantined, the three of us were then left to face the wearisome night on a bench near the sergeant's office. I didn't want to sleep. However, I knew sleep would eventually overcome me. Meanwhile I talked to my companions. At first the Italian was most agitated, so I gave him a chance to simmer down.

Herman, the Dutchman, said he was backpacking through Africa. He wanted to get away to open spaces because he felt that Holland was simply too crowded. Besides, his girlfriend was working as a volunteer in a Zambian leprosarium and he felt he would like to give her a pleasant surprise. It was he who had got the surprise. She had fallen 'head over the heels' in love with a fellow volunteer, an Irish doctor. She had intended to break the news to him when she got back to Holland. As he dwelt upon it, he began to develop a morose hangdog look.

I urged him not to completely lose hope. Oftentimes, being a couple of whites isolated in the African bush does strange things to people's perceptions. Maybe, on returning to Holland, things would take on a completely different complexion for her. I'd seen it happen more than once.

'I hope you're right.'

'Do you think our luggage is safe?' I asked, in an effort to distract him from his pain.

'Oh, I could lose everything they've got locked up there and survive with this backpack.' He then lay down on the floor and, using the pack for a pillow, sought refuge from weariness and pain in sleep.

The Italian was not likely to fall asleep for a time. I learned that his name was Dino Restelli, an electrical engineer, in West Africa on business and on a very tight schedule. He couldn't afford a hitch. Hence his disquiet at our present predicament.

'I didn't know that you needed a visa, if you were the transit *passeggero*,' he complained again. 'You can tell me what the perhaps English word for *passeggero* is?'

'Passenger.'

'O stupido!'

'And to tell you the truth, Dino, I don't think you need a visa, strictly speaking.'

'Then what goes on here?'

'I guess the government wants customers for its hotels, or some such thing. Foreign currency, you know.'

'But if we go to the hotel, we go to the bed and then we must to get up immediately.'

'Quite so.'

'O santa pace!'

After a pause Dino asked, 'What do you do for a living?'

'I'm a priest.'

'A Catholic priest?'

'Yes.'

'I'm a Catholic too.'

'I thought you might be.'

'I'm not the very good Catholic, but a Catholic nevertheless. After all, what else is there to be? God is a Catholic.'

I could almost hear Martin Luther, John Calvin, and John Knox – not to speak of Lord Buddha and Mohammed – turn collectively in their graves.

'I go to Mass for Christmas and how you say …?'

'Easter?'

'Yes, for Easter. But I send my wife and kids to church every Sunday and obligation day. *Si signore*, I'm very strict about that. My wife she do all the praying for me. But I think there is something wrong with the church in Italy. The priests are too distant. Their idea is to try to be holy like the alabaster angels behind the glass with lights and flowers around them. They're not in this world. They're not … human,' he found the exact word he wanted. 'I find it difficult to explain.'

'You explain yourself very well.'

'I like priests to be human, like Papa Wojtyla, he go among the people, he ski, in *somma* he's got *pantaloni*, he's got the flesh and the blood.'

'I like Paul VI too.'

'No, Paulo Sexto was far away, like the angel, not human.'

'I have to disagree. I thought he was shy, yet I sensed a genuinely concerned man. But I could understand you getting the impression you did, since he was something of an introvert. I have to tell you something that a Cardinal I chanced to meet once told me about the difference between John XXIII and Paul VI – this is a little footnote to history. According to him, John was an incurable optimist and, even when things were going badly, thought they were going marvellously. Paul was the opposite. An anxious man who, even when things were going well, felt they were going awry. That's by the way.'

'You know my teacher when I go to school is a priest, Don Molinari. He was a man.'

'You didn't happen to go to a Salesian school, did you?'

'How you guess?'

'They're involved a lot in technical education.'

'Don Molinari play football with us and he like to tell many jokes. He like a cognac too! He was human. You are a *Salesiano*?'

'Yes.'

'*Viva Don Bosco!*'

'*Eviva!*'

'Look, I have only one principle in life,' said Dino, becoming grave, 'and that is love your next.'

That sounded familiar.

Regarding me with a dubious half-smile, he said, 'Ah, I know you are thinking about my burst-out with the African back there. You are thinking I am the racist.'

'Actually, I was focusing on what you were saying. Now that you mention it though, what you said wasn't exactly flattering.'

'I didn't mean anythin. Just got a bit excited and speak the mind. There is no malice.'

'Maybe you should go back and tell the inspector that his country isn't half-assed.'

At this he smiled wanly.

GOD IS A CATHOLIC

Dino was still talking when I started to droop. Not surprisingly I had my recurring Kafkaesque airport dream. I'm about to board a plane, but where is that ticket? Nowhere to be found. A friend supposes that I left it at the coffee counter and rushes off to fetch it. I wait and wait in vain. The friend never returns. I go to the coffee counter. There is no longer a coffee counter. An airport official in a dark uniform with gold braiding approaches me, 'Sir, did you by any chance misplace a ticket?' 'Yes, yes,' I reply eagerly. 'I'll be right back with it.' I almost weep with sheer relief. There's no time to lose. He returns beaming and hands me the ticket. I turn to the check-in counter where I am now standing to pick up the leather bag containing my passport that I have left down momentarily. It's gone.' And so the concatenation of mishaps continues. As I free one foot from the nightmarish quicksands, the other sinks into the slime and holds me fast.

I awake with a shudder, mightily relieved that it was all only a dream, yet the negative feelings still weigh heavily upon my spirits. The shudder is not from the cold, because it is sweltering. Herman is still sleeping with his head resting on his precious backpack. Dino's dark curls sink slowly to his chest and then jerk upright of a sudden.

I arouse the sleepers. The time for departure is fast approaching. No sign of our passports being returned. Anxiety mounts by the second. The office of the sergeant is locked and he is nowhere in sight. The departing aircraft is virtually revving up on the tarmac, when suspense snaps with the breathless appearance of the sergeant, bleary-eyed and stubbled. We are lucky. He hurriedly summons us to the office.

'Herman Kanters?'

'Here.' Herman was handed his passport and made haste to the plane.

'James O'Halloran?'

'That's me.'

'You Irish?'

'Yes.'

'Fr Murphy is my old teacher,' says he with a smile as he hands me my passport.

'That's nice. Thank you. And the luggage?'

'Loaded.'

'See you on board, Dino,' I say, hastily following Herman. Good old Fr Murphy. I guess I owe you.

I complete the formalities and am about to leave the departure lounge when something catches my eye. It is the hapless Dino inside an office remonstrating with his interrogator of the night before. The inspector sits, face tinged with scorn, languidly leafing through a passport.

The aircraft roars off into the sultry sky – without Dino. But there is another flight in a week's time!

Music and Dissonance

It was early 1991 and I found myself in a remote village in Sierra Leone, giving sessions on community building. In many ways it was like pushing on an open door because the people were quite community minded.

When I first arrived, the inhabitants of the village had vague notions about why I was there and, since I was white, presumed it was for some beneficent purpose. In this they were correct, but it wasn't beneficent in a way they expected. We gathered in a centre with thatched roof and slatted walls; inside it was packed with adults, while from outside a crowd of children peered in through the slats with great liquid eyes. I was soon peppered with requests for a new school building, medical centre, football pitch, palm oil press...

A friend James, who had accompanied me from the distant mission centre, explained that I didn't have the means to supply these things. Necessary though they might be, providing them was not within my remit. I came with no big money bag. I had, however, a message that was most important. We would share together, not on building walls, but on how we might build up, and enrich, community. To my amazement, a sympathetic sigh of appreciation, even relief, seemed to emanate from the gathering. They had come to do battle for material rewards with what they thought to be an affluent white man, only to discover that something quite other was on offer. At that moment a scene from the Bible came to mind. It was that of Peter and John being accosted by a beggar at the gate of the Temple and Peter saying to him, 'Silver and gold I have none, but what I have I give unto you. Arise and walk!' In the event, the timing and subject matter of the session were 'unfortunately' to prove providential.

Mind you, it wasn't the first time that a visit of mine provoked great expectations. In yet another Sierra Leonean village I had entered a few years previously, I had a similar experience. A court was in session under a mango tree, the judge being a venerable *alhajji* – a Muslim who'd done the *hajj*, or great pilgrimage to Mecca – in flowing robe and tasselled fez. Although the session seemed to be embroiled in a question of mammy palaver, the participants ceased deliberations momentarily to welcome me.

'How de body?' The judge greeted me in the customary fashion.

'De body fine,' I returned the greeting. 'How you own body?'

'Fine, thank you.' And then he continued, 'Sah, I don't know which side you come out, Russia or de United States, but we need de hospital here one time.' The *alhajji* was nothing if not direct. I couldn't help but smile at the influence he attributed to me – if you weren't careful it could be quite intoxicating.

But to get back to our first village. On the subject of community, the sharing was rich – the participants didn't need convincing on the necessity of relationships. But where the bonding really took place was in the sharing of goat's meat, yam, palm wine, conversation and laughter following the session. Cohesion is not a matter of fine talk; it happens in simple ways.

At this meal, the wise old chief, again a Muslim in flowing robes and tasselled fez, expressing his satisfaction at the session and the celebratory meal, made this enlightened statement: 'I'd like to thank Baba and all who took part in the proceedings. I am the chief in this village; some of my people are Muslim, some Christian, but it is necessary that we all pull together. You are all my people. I am concerned for the good of all. Today has been very helpful.' If this wisdom only prevailed in the great power centres of the world, what a difference it would make.

I was the only white man in this remote village and, from what happened, I concluded the appearance of someone of my colour was a rare event. For the children gathered around, gazing at me in wonder. They plucked gently at the hair on my arms – Africans don't have hair on their arms. One little lad rubbed my pale arm vigorously to uncover the black underneath. When it did not appear and the reality dawned, his eyes became great saucers and he laughed heartily. Worse still, another tot, on seeing this bogeyman, hid behind his mother's skirts with a look of terror on his

MUSIC AND DISSONANCE

face and commenced to whimper. The smiling, yet embarrassed, mother sought to pacify him.

When I produced my camera, everyone wanted to be photographed. I happily obliged until the films ran out. Very often people in Africa are reluctant to have their picture taken. They believe that their spirit is somehow diminished in the process.

Before leaving the village, I saw dubious characters in quasi-military uniform around the place. I got the feeling that they had crossed the border from Liberia where Charles Taylor, and others, were waging their brutal war. A favourite 'pastime' was cutting limbs off people. Victims were cynically asked whether they wanted long or short sleeves, meaning did they want their arms cut off at the elbows or the wrists.

I think my hunch about the soldiers was correct because a week later rebels from the Revolutionary United Front under Fodah Sankoh crossed over the Liberian border and extended that awful war into Sierra Leone. And so began a ten-year civil conflict destined to leave 75,000 Sierra Leoneans dead and visit unspeakable atrocities upon good people: heads of community leaders cut off and put on stakes, boy soldiers forced to kill members of their own families – to harden them for battle – limbs severed, pillage and rape.

On arrival, these thugs soon came to the mission where my friend James worked and demanded that he join them. He resolutely refused, saying he was needed on the mission and that, as an only son, he had to take care of an aged mother. Besides, he was a man of peace. Sadly he, who had made the music of unity and love in life, was summarily shot in the head. I had just left a few days before and was devastated by the news. In my desolation, I found solace in recalling the tolerant aspirations of the wise old chief. As long as there were people who voiced those sentiments, there was hope for Africa, hope for the world. I have no doubt but that his words were a beacon in the dark years that were to follow. Where James was concerned, I regretted not being able to say, 'Arise and walk!'

Did the head of the wise old chief end up on a stake? His fate was obscured in the confusion and chaos of war.

When I eventually left Sierra Leone with a heavy heart for my next African destination, troops of the national army were guarding the plane as it took off. The capital, Freetown, was itself under threat.

Stella

I would often see Stella in the teeming thoroughfare. Even before I got to know her personally. She was young and attractive and smiling, had a cheerful word for everyone, but was disabled. Not too severely. Splayed feet it was. Which was why she sat begging.

People were generous with her. Europeans would approach almost surreptitiously with an embarrassed, even guilty, expression and slip a coin without looking at her. This amused Stella, yet she knew how to manipulate the situation. Seeing her as an equal, fellow Africans shared with her in a most natural fashion. And the harder times were, the more generous they became.

I myself took to chatting with her, and I too could help without feeling awkward. I had been in Africa a long while.

At times she ribbed me unmercifully, 'Jim, why I no beautiful like you white people?'

'My, you are getting ambitious,' I joined the charade.

'Why I have dis crinkly hair and dis li'l button nose?'

'You're very ugly really.'

'I like to have straight yellow hair an' pearly white skin an' nice shape nose – wid a point,' here she stole a cunning glance at me.

'Too bad, Stella, you can't and that's that.'

'Den your lips is red an' your eyes is blue. My lips is red too [she plastered them with lipstick] but the blue paint hurt my eyes stop me see!' Then she would laugh long and uproariously.

A favourite ploy of hers, when speaking with me, was to call out to a passing acquaintance, somewhat darker than herself, 'Who dat black man?' She knew this never failed to entertain and, when the bemused fellow had gone, would ask, 'What dat saying 'bout de pot an' de kettle?'

Work reasons forced me to absent myself from Baytown for quite some time. On my return I was in for a rude shock. Stella was wasting away. The hair was dull and unkempt, the eyes dimmed, her colour ashen.

Not having the energy to speak, she said simply, 'I sick, Jim.'
'Didn't you go to hospital?'
'Dey have no medicine.'

I approached the Sisters of Charity and they came to her rescue. A medical examination showed that she was suffering from tuberculosis. She was given a neat little room at the convent and lay there wanly between immaculate sheets.

With infinite dedication, much medication and many a bowl of delicate chicken broth, the nuns nursed Stella back to health and strength. I knew she was on the mend the day she accosted me with 'Why you look so sick? You like to be black same as me?'

In the later stages of her recuperation, she began to learn dressmaking. The sisters, who had her future in mind, did not want her to go on the street begging again.

But for all that, Stella seemed to be growing restive. Then one day she dropped her bombshell, 'I want to go out an' beg now.'

Sister Evangelista's face fell and she looked at her in blank disbelief, 'You what?!'

'I want to go out an' beg.'

'That's what I thought you said. What on earth for? You've got a room, food, a skill, some money. You don't want to throw all that away, do you?'

Stella pouted, 'I no happy.'

'Not happy! You'd rather shame yourself sitting by the side of the street begging.'

Stella looked bewildered.

'No, my girl, we haven't gone to all this trouble for you to go back on the street again, have we? Don't be ridiculous.'

Stella was silent.

'Go away and think again,' Evangelista urged.

After a lengthy, sullen pause, Stella shuffled out.

Evangelista, reinserting a curler that had slipped out from under her veil, sought out Genevieve. Genevieve was appalled. Go back on the streets! The ingratitude of it! How could she even dream of it? Sooner or later, of course, some irresponsible good-for-nothing would take advantage of her and make her pregnant. Ah well, it would be her own doing. Let it be upon her own head if she couldn't see sense.

'What is sense?' philosophically interposed Edel, a lively young nun from the West of Ireland with a headful of newfangled ideas.

'Sister Edel, if you'd obey the Holy Father and wear your veil instead of asking such silly questions, you'd be much better off,' retorted Genevieve.

'Mind you, veils have their uses,' Edel replied (Evangelista went crimson), 'but, Genevieve dear, even St Paul only insists on women having their heads covered in church.'

'And there you are having a go at St Paul again. I know you're no fan of his with all your women's lib nonsense.'

'If you want my opinion –'

'Not specially.'

'If you want my opinion,' persevered Edel, 'I don't think God herself would agree with everything St Paul had to say about women.'

Genevieve became simultaneously purple and speechless.

Grasping both of them by an arm, Evangelista shepherded them speedily away to evening prayer. As she went, Edel gave an ankle a slight wrench because of a high heel.

Day by day the once good-humoured Stella became more fractious and difficult. 'She's complaining about the food now,' Genevieve was quite beside herself. 'She'd rather have her rice swimming in palm oil and be burning her mouth off with peppers.'

And still the girl continued her slide downward from being extremely difficult to becoming utterly impossible.

'Bloody hell! Get out and beg then!' yelled Evangelista at last.

'Evangelista!' gently chided the surprised Genevieve. Edel giggled.

With a face like a thunder-cloud Stella betook herself laboriously from the convent.

Overcome with a mixture of anger and guilt, Evangelista declared, 'There's gratitude for you. Ah well, that's that.'

But that was not that. Indeed it wasn't too long before the vivacious Stella of old returned to see the nuns as though a harsh word had never been uttered between them. She showed her takings for the day. Eight dollars. 'Why, that's twice what primary teachers earn,' noted Genevieve.

'I bring you some nice cream buns,' said Stella. 'I know Sister Evangelista have de sweet teeth.'

At about that time I had to leave Baytown once more, for an entire year. Stella slipped from my mind. On my return I soon saw her at the accustomed spot by the cathedral. She had a baby in her arms. Yes, she had met the irresponsible good-for-nothing who took advantage of her.

On seeing me, she held up the baby with a rapturous smile and then hugged it to her breast.

I approached and offered her a handkerchief, 'Wipe your mouth, Stella, it's all smeared with palm oil.'

Moonstruck

I awoke suddenly in the dark heart of Africa. A shaft of peaceful moonlight streamed through the window, ending in a pool on the earthen floor. But the night was not peaceful. Terrified shouts, screams, ululating and whistles shattered the night from amid the mud huts of the nearby village – a cacophony that was significantly augmented by an ear-splitting percussion of drums, castanets, pots and pans, saucepan lids … I had obviously been awakened by this clamour.

I dashed outside into the moonlit compound. Surveyed the village and surrounding bush. No smoke. No fire. So it was not one of those fearsome bush fires that can devour all that stands in its way. What, I wondered in my panic – I was shaking all over – was causing this commotion?

It was then that the moon caught my attention. It stood in the sky like a burnished shield, but that shield was partially obscured. An eclipse of the moon was in progress. I hadn't been alerted to this because I had spent some weeks in remote areas where news often doesn't penetrate.

I watched the whole eclipse in awe while still remaining baffled by the uproar. But, once it had passed, there was a remarkable change. The mayhem was replaced by sounds of merriment – cries of delight, singing, drumming and dancing – fuelled, no doubt, by draughts of native beer. The jollifications continued long into the night; indeed they did not cease until the first rays of daylight fingered the horizon and the muezzin thumped his deep-sounding drum while beginning his chant to arouse his Islamic brethren for prayer.

Yet the quandary remained as to the explanation of the distress that preceded the celebrations. I was in Mende country in Sierra Leone, so I decided to consult a wise Mende man.

'You see,' he explained, 'we Mende people have de belief dat all de life come from de moon. When de evil spirits attack de moon, like last night, we must to frighten dem away. When dey go, we make plenty party.'

It all, of course, made perfect sense. The moon was a great source of joy. In places where you didn't pollute the darkness with electricity, nights with a full moon were a gift. On those occasions, people could make merry, tell stories, cement relationships. In a word: build community. Given these circumstances, it is understandable that the moon is seen as the source of life. After all, life is about relationships.

If, then, you find yourselves among the Mendes on a moonlit night, during an eclipse, you are likely to have the experience I had. They will sally forth with their dissonant symphony of noise to drive away the evil spirits that are trying to destroy the source of all life, as they have done for eons. They always succeed, so what more proof is needed?

And they always celebrate. Are they not giving us an invaluable lesson as to how to confront the numerous ogres that menace life?

The Sun Sets

The word had been going around for days. A Young International Voluntary Service member James Pike would address the annual Oxbridge Boat Race Dinner on the evening of Saturday, 9 March. On his mother's side he was the direct descendant of a renowned English Prime Minister. Old Oxonians and Cantabrigians looked forward eagerly to the event, for he was a brilliant young man, who at the moment was one of the many volunteers serving in the little African country of Zongoland that was soon to become independent. It was to be an all-male gathering and ties were of course obligatory. Fr O'Connell, a Roman Catholic priest who had done a smattering of studies at Oxford, was roped in to say grace, in Latin. Some eyebrows were raised at his inclusion. Did postgraduate studies provide sufficient credentials? Did the reverend ever hear the music of leather on willow down in the parks? Punt on the dreamy Isis? Or sport a valiant rose at Finals?

Anyway, come the evening in question, there he was, large as life, declaring '*Benedicite* ...' as he said grace over the reverently bowed heads of assorted Christians, atheists and agnostics.

Fr O'Connell found himself at table with three volunteers. These attacked their shrimp cocktail with relish. One was a pleasant young man with long, carefully groomed black hair and a delicate aquiline nose. He was actually wearing an academic gown. The second was small, fair-haired and curt. The third a big fellow with large thick-lens spectacles that gave him a distinctively owlish look.

'Which colleges did you go to lads?' asked Fr O'Connell amiably.

'I was at Balliol,' said the pleasant young man. 'Spent three jolly years there. Too jolly I suppose. Came away with a gentleman's third, and that only after vivas!'

'And I came away with a first from Magdalen,' said the fair-haired fellow bluntly, and, of course, in the worst possible taste.

'I'm the exception, I dare say. I was at King's, Cambridge,' said the big owlish man. But his light blue tie had betrayed him anyway. He added nothing about firsts or thirds.

'You didn't sing in the renowned choir by any chance?' asked the agreeable young man. 'I just adored listening to them on Christmas Eve.'

'Actually, I'm quite fond of singing and reckoned reasonably good at it, but I'm agnostic.'

'Oh, that would be something of an obstacle, I dare say ... And yourself reverend?' the pleasant young man continued.

'Oh me, I spent an enjoyable year doing the Dip. Ed. down in Norham Gardens.'

'Enjoyable?' remarked the curt fellow.

'Yes, the amber autumn I will never forget, or the lights shining through the glorious stained-glass windows of college chapels as I cycled home in the dark after a day's lectures. Sometimes you could hear the strains of an organ thundering from within. Then I was fortunate to have this most wonderful tutor, a Mr Loukes, who gave me some of the greatest advice I ever got about education.' Fr O'Connell stopped, leaving his companions with spoons poised and mouths slightly ajar. He had a sense of the dramatic.

'Well, aren't you going to tell us what his advice was?' asked the curt fellow after a considerable pause.

'Oh yes, "Remember, James," says he, "that when you are talking to students you have no guarantee that they are learning anything. Listening is the rarest of arts, you know. Talkers abound, but listeners are something of an endangered species. However, if you put your students to work, you definitely know that they are learning something. I would keep exposition to a minimum and rather get pupils working. And don't be afraid to jolt the system by letting them help each other in groups. I think the whole paranoia over copying is grossly exaggerated. It reflects – and serves the needs of – an individualistic and unhealthily competitive society in my view. We pedagogues are supposed to be preparing people for life, not manufacturing automatons for a technological age".'

'Fascinating,' said the large owlish man.

THE SUN SETS

'Now if you think about it,' continued Fr O'Connell, 'that put the ideas of the abstruse Paulo Freire in a nutshell. Involve students actively in their own education. Stimulate them to think for themselves. Which is what education is about.'

'Quite,' they agreed and somehow left it at that.

'Looking around here,' Fr O'Connell was taking up the slack again, 'you'd think Oxbridge men were running Zongoland. There's so many of them.'

'Aren't we?' asked the pleasant young man archly.

A recording of the Boat Race that had taken place earlier that day was being played and the plummy voice of John Snagg could be heard above the buzz of conversation. '... coming towards the Fulham end there's nothing between the boats ... Cambridge may have a slight advantage ... both crews are rowing sweetly as they come past the black buoy ... Cambridge riding the rough water well ... the two teams on thirty-six strokes a minute ... it's neck and neck ... wonderful clarity of rowing by both teams ... good rhythm ... very little check as they pick up the catch ... no prospect of clear water in sight ...'

The Governor General, Sir Horace Cattermole, was seated at the principal table with two top civil servants, Sir Patrick fFrench Johnson and Sir Crispin Hope Soames. A place had also been reserved there for the guest of honour, Mr James Pike, but he had elected to sit with some fellow volunteers. Sir Horace could see the group engaged in animated conversation. He noticed that young James Pike was dressed in a safari suit. No tie. Tut! Tut! Obviously an unconventional young man. Needed a little more time to slip into the mould.

Sir Crispin was Vice-Chancellor of the University of Zongoland and a tall donnish man with a dishevelled mop of silver hair and eyes that looked distant and diminished behind thick spectacles. A brilliant scholar, he sometimes relaxed by reading classical Greek authors. He had a reputation for being dreadfully absent-minded. On one occasion he was perusing the Iliad in a bank queue and on arrival at the counter tried to return the volume to the cashier and wondered why the obtuse librarian was creating problems.

Sir Patrick on the other hand was a rather mediocre soul, who had acquired his title for plodding fidelity in the colonial service. His appearance was bloated and he wore a morose, hangdog expression.

'And now Zongoland is to get its independence,' Sir Patrick was moaning.

'Yes,' replied Sir Crispin, 'I see Councillor Gamongo said in the Assembly the other day that – and I quote – "Zongoland must have its independence as soon as possible next year".'

'Umph, how about the 1st of January?' volunteered Sir Horace.

'Jolly good, Sir Horace,' cried Crispin, 'jolly, jolly good', laughing heartily and slapping his thigh. Not a hint of a smile touched the face of the melancholy Sir Patrick. 'As soon as possible next year,' chortled Sir Crispin, 'why not the 1st of January … why not indeed … jolly good.'

When Sir Crispin had subsided, Sir Patrick continued, 'Gentlemen, these people aren't ready for independence. There is no way they will be able to get on without us. Nor were they ready in Kenya, the Rhodesias – Smithy did his best to stop the rot there – Malawi, Bechuanaland or Basutoland. I've seen it all. As each one folded, I was driven further afield. Bearing the white man's burden has been my life. It wasn't a bad life,' he mused growing misty-eyed. 'How I loved to sit of an evening, watch the sky ablaze behind gently waving palms, and unwind with a good stiff sundowner –'

'Or two!' interposed Sir Crispin.

Sir Patrick chose to ignore the remark. 'After dinner, like a character – I believe it was in one of Maugham's stories – I'd pour over outdated copies of *The Times* from England, devouring every tiny bit of news and scandal, although, to tell the truth, England was the last place I wanted to be. Odd that, when you come to think of it. Probably end my days in a London flat now. Looking out on those blasted grey November days.'

'Not to speak of the same possibility in September, October, December, January, or, for that matter, July,' added Sir Crispin.

'Umph, you're a barrel of fun,' observed Sir Patrick.

THE SUN SETS

'Sorry, old chap, didn't mean to depress you.'

'Oh cheer up, Paddy,' declared a boyant Sir Horace, 'there's still Tristan de Cunha and St Helena left.'

'Yes,' replied Sir Patrick, 'I seem to remember that someone else had a whale of a time on St Helena. No, gentlemen, the sun is now setting on the British Empire with a bang,' he finished rather incongruously.

And adverting to Northern Ireland, Fr O'Connell, who had overheard snatches of this conversation from where he sat, thought, There is even a worm in the heart of the empire, Sir Patrick.

The Boat Race was concluding, so someone turned the volume right up.

'Once saw the Boat Race from the air,' remarked Sir Patrick. 'Spiffing good view.'

'The exhausted crews are approaching the finish ... have given it their all,' John Snagg was growing really excited ... 'nothing in it at all ... depends on which team can find the heart and hand for a final surge ... they are striving might and main ... it's Oxford ... it's going to be Oxford ... yes, it's the dark blues ... but, my goodness, only by inches in the most exciting Boat Race for years.'

A clipped 'hurrah' from the Oxford men greeted the victory in a civilised, non-bragging way. Those of their number who hadn't known the result were somewhat more animated. The Cantabrigians present generously offered congratulations to the 'foe'. 'Jolly good show, Sir Crispin,' declared Sir Horace offering him a hand. Frankly, the volunteers didn't seem to *give* a damn either way. When the excitement, such as it was, faded and conversation returned to normal levels, people began to give anticipatory glances in the direction of Mr James Pike.

Clink! Clink! Clink!

Someone was tapping a glass. It was Harold Thompson, the MC for the evening. 'Ladies and gentlemen –' A roar of laughter. 'I mean gentlemen of course. It rather reminds me of the time that members of ... shall we say the distaff side ... were first allowed into Oxford. There was a venerable and stately professor who did not at all agree with the policy, yet was forced to grin and bear it, so to speak. Afterwards, when he came lecturing to mixed audiences, he would customarily begin by saying, "Gentlemen," and proceed to ostensibly ignore all the ladies present. It is related that on one occasion he arrived to find a hall full of ladies with only one man in their midst, whereupon he dutifully began his lecture with a reverential "Sir," making a slight bow in the direction of the solitary male. Finally there arrived the inevitable day when he found himself confronted with females only. As you can imagine the situation had actually been engineered by the students to see how he would confront the dilemma. Well, he placed his lecture notes on the lectern and surveyed the whole room from his vantage point on the rostrum. 'Ah, nobody heah today!' he noted and, gathering up his notes, sailed majestically out of the hall with robes billowing behind:

>Like a stately ship
>Of Tarsus, bound for th'isles
>Of Javan or Gadire.

as Milton would put it.'

'Bully for you, Harold,' cried an amused Sir Horace and others joined in the mirth.

'And now we come to the highlight of our evening,' said Harold. 'We shall be addressed by Mr James Pike – his modesty precludes me from giving him his proper title of "The Right Honourable James Pike". He is, as you already know, a direct descendant on his mother's side of a great parliamentarian and Prime Minister of England. Indeed following the sure instincts of his noble forebear, James is serving Queen and country – and Zongoland of course – as a volunteer. Gentlemen, without more ado, I give you Mr James Pike.'

The applause was loud, especially from those volunteers present. The Governor General, Sir Horace, lit his pipe and visibly relaxed into his chair, his face aglow with anticipatory pleasure. James ceased conversing with his companions, studiously removed his serviette, dabbed his mouth with it and rose from his chair.

'Gentlemen,' he began tentatively, and his voice sounded unexpectedly high-pitched, 'I'm deeply honoured to be asked to

THE SUN SETS

address this illustrious gathering here this evening. As you know, or perhaps you don't, we volunteers have our deprivations. So on behalf of all my fellows I should like to thank you for having furnished us with at least one hearty meal. I believe we did it justice.'

This sally brought its share of laughter and applause, especially from the volunteers. 'Heah! Heah! James,' they cried.

'Once again I thank you very much,' said the budding orator – and took his seat.

For a moment there was a stunned silence. Sir Horace sat with poised disbelieving pipe. Harold, the MC, fidgeted and a sour look briefly washed over his face.

'Is that all there is?' muttered Sir Crispin. 'Shorter even than Gettysburg.'

The volunteers laughed, cheered and applauded. The others clapped perfunctorily.

'The MC's introduction exceeded the keynote speech by a long shot,' sniffed Sir Patrick.

A smile played on the lips of Fr O'Connell.

'Time for cigars and port, gentlemen,' announced an ebullient Sir Horace with stiff upper lip.

The guests had an earlier night than expected.

Discovery

Together with a group of Zambians I jumped aboard the powerful truck and set out for the source of the Zambezi. I travelled up front with Mulenga, the driver, while behind there was a clatter of noisy boys who usually congregated round the remote Catholic Mission of Ikelenge. With camera boldly slung over shoulder, in case a marauding lion had to be 'shot', and wearing a khaki, 'Out-of-Africa' suit, I was in a sense fulfilling a fantasy deeply rooted in childhood.

Long ago I had been through savannahs like these with all their lurking dangers. It was in the company of a toupeed Henry Morton Stanley, played by Spencer Tracy, at the Gaiety Cinema, Callan, Ireland, in the 1940s. For a few hours that were dramatically transformed into months I suffered all the renowned explorer's travails of hunger, thirst, weariness, malaria, fractious carriers and lethal wildlife as he searched for the almost mystical David Livingstone. I could still recall that climactic scene where Stanley strides up to the remote figure, extends a hand and utters those immortal words: 'Dr Livingstone I presume?' So shattering was the journey, so uncertain the achievement of its goal and so much did one empathise with the incomparable acting of Tracy that one could fully understand the reaction of a well-known local 'character' who blurted out, 'Begob, let's all go up and shake hands with the fella.' Such audience participation was not uncommon at the Gaiety.

The safari by lorry was a breeze in comparison. We sped through stately grasses along the laterite road that had been painted a deep gold by recent rains. Here and there scarlet flamboyants laughed together with sunny, yellow-blossomed markhemia and gladdened the heart. It wasn't long until we arrived at the edge of a dark wood. Deep within lay the source of the mighty Zambezi.

With an air of expectation we dismounted from the lorry and,

DISCOVERY

led by Mulenga, plunged into the forest. It was soggy under foot, because, although the sky was limpid today, it was the rainy season. My sturdy boots sank deep into the mouldering leaves. After a while the heat and darkness grew oppressive. I found a soaked shirt clinging tenaciously to my back as sweat trickled down my forehead and burned the corners of my eyes. And the thirst!

O, for a draught of vintage! that hath been
Cool'd a long age in the deep-delvéd earth.

I echoed the ardent sentiments of Keats. No canteen of water dangled at my side. Stanley or Livingstone would never have been guilty of such an omission. Nothing daunted, like those intrepid explorers, I trudged on in the footsteps of Mulenga and his noisy horde.

It was dark and eerie. One imagined the ghostly eyes of Conradian adventurers, who had succumbed to blackwater fever, peering malevolently from among the trees. Something indefinable about the place oppressed. Mosquitoes drilled at my ears. How any escaped the spiders I would never know, for practically at every step a web ensnared my face. These I would wipe away, while being haunted by the vision of tarantulas, and stumble on. Occasionally a moist shaft of light, laden with the rainbow wings of insects and now glistening webs, would break through. I stood gasping for a moment and took in the beauty. High above there was the querulous cry of a fish eagle. 'Where there's a fish eagle there must be water,' I said, stating the obvious. From its eyrie in the sky it was, perhaps, surveying at a glance the upper reaches of the Zambezi that took Livingstone arduous weeks to explore. Breathing easily once more, I plodded on.

Truth to tell, it wasn't long until I heard an excited shout up ahead. They had come upon the source. Now I would discover it. Pulling out my camera, I scurried up to join them. The group encircled a pool. Then Mulenga noted water trickling into the pool. False alarm. We were hot on the trail, however, and within a short distance there it was, the genesis of that prostrate giant – the Zambezi. If in your mind's eye you see a vigorous spring, gushing forth from the remote depths of the earth, forget it. My first reaction was one of profound disappointment, but it quickly gave way to admiration and awe. There at my feet lay a most unimpressive brackish pool embedded in a mass of fallen leaves. It reminded me of a listless puddle on a remote country road after rains. And to think that a thousand miles from here this puddle would be transformed into the everlasting roar of the colossal Victoria Falls, whose mere spray, 'the smoke that thunders', surged for about one thousand feet into the air. It truly baffled the mind. I photographed the place from every possible angle. Lined up the members of my expedition on the spot so as to freeze the historic moment forever. Had my own picture taken, fingers lightly touching the Grailish waters.

The gaggle of boys rushed mindlessly away. No sense of occasion. As for me, I stood rooted to the sacred spot, musing. Symphonic music played in my head. I felt as Speke must have done when he discovered Lake Victoria, or 'stout Cortez', or whoever:

> ... when with eagle eyes
> He stared at the Pacific – and all his men
> Looked at each other with a wild surmise –
> Silent, upon a peak in Darien.

Now there was a fascinating thought. Cortez was not the first to discover the Pacific and surely Keats must have known this. But did it really matter? Wasn't Cortez' experience unique for him? Discovery wasn't just a monopoly of Balboa.

As I came down to earth from these grand reveries, I found that Mulenga had been studying me in silence all the while with an enigmatic smile on his face.

'Mulenga,' I confided reverently, 'Livingstone was the first person to discover the upper reaches of the Zambezi and the Victoria Falls, you know.'

'Well, actually,' a smiling Mulenga replied softly and with great politeness, 'our people knew they were here all the time.'

'Hmmm ... yes ... will we go back to the truck?'

Loath to let Mulenga's words intrude upon my childhood fantasy, I walked back to the lorry with a Livingstonian spring in my step. As I emerged from the gloom of the forest and blinked, I saw that all the boys had lined up to form a welcoming party cum guard of honour. We regarded each other in silence. Then a solemn-faced Kalumba, normally an imp, came and presented me with a bouquet of green ferns. 'Sorry there are no flowers about here,' he apologised.

I was truly perplexed. 'What is the meaning of the gesture?' I inquired of Mulenga. With a twinkle in his eye, he replied, 'You know the sort of thing ... something like victors being crowned with laurels.'

Then an obviously tutored Kalumba held out his hand and said, 'Dr Livingstone I presume?'

At this, the whole party fell about the place in helpless laughter. And with my self-important bubble burst what was left for me but to do the same.

The Vulture

The vulture wheeled about in the pale blue sky. So pale as to be virtually non-existent. Far below there lay a tropical scene heightened by the bright morning sunlight. Palm, paw-paw, cotton, cola, elephant grass and indeterminate bush all combined to weave a luxuriant carpet. The sun glanced off a waterfall and then laughed along a stream that flowed from it. Little wisps of mist from the harmattan still lingered in the folds of the gentle hills.

To the east grey-white smoke arose from a bush fire as the tongues of flame devoured the undergrowth. The vulture marked well the birds and animals fleeing in terror before the inferno.

From a distance too a farmer viewed the fire apprehensively as he thus prepared his land for cultivation. His fear was grounded in many a charred and gutted West African village.

On the west side of the scene, unrolled beneath the vulture, there was a higgledy-piggledy, populous town. Crowds of people were wending their way towards, and speedily filling, an arena where a show was obviously in progress. The flowing garbs were vibrant: blues, yellows, greens, reds and mottled versions of these created a large moving and swirling flower garden.

The whole panorama was bejewelled with sparkling zinc roofs, massed together treasure-like in the town, sparse yet still more welcome in the open country.

But the laser eyes of the circling vulture were unimpressed by all this glory. Its unblinking look had for hours been transfixed by a yellow Toyota pick-up, parked beside one of those glittering roofs. Its interest now quickened. A burly man sat into the vehicle, backed somewhat, and then roared speedily away in a broad arc. When the dust settled, a cuddly ginger cat lay with the life just crushed out of it. It had unfortunately sought refuge beneath the Toyota very early in the morning from the chill of the harmattan.

Immediately the vulture plummeted with whirring feathers from its great height. And as the beautiful and burgeoning scene below rushed towards it, the scavenger dived unerringly upon that grim russet speck of lifelessness.

Heart in Hand

Conall McEvoy shook uncontrollably and was overwhelmed by weakness. Even the mere action of raising a glass of water to his lips left him utterly prostrated. He felt nausea and a strange tingling in his hands and feet. At one moment he burned with heat, at the next he was bathed in cold sweat. He vomited to the point where there was nothing left to come up, and his whole frame was racked by an empty retching that yielded only rheum.

Throughout the long, hot night he lay suffering beneath his claustrophobic mosquito net, except for the moments when he struggled to the bathroom, grasping a storm lamp. As he entered, a cloud of mosquitoes came out to meet him. Brushing them aside with a weary hand, he thought ruefully that they were probably the cause of his present anguish.

Never had he been so relieved to see the first glimmer of an approaching day. With swirling head he made his way to Paul's room and knocked on the door. Paul was the priest in charge of the little West African mission station where Conall, himself a seminarist, was getting a couple of years experience before going back to Ireland to finish his studies for the priesthood. Paul was snoring. Conall hesitated before knocking again, because his companion worked hard and badly needed his night's sleep. But, then, he really did feel wretched, so he rapped loudly on the door.

'Yes?' a startled voice answered from within.

'Paul, I'm not feelin very well.'

'That you, Conall?' Paul was still somewhat disoriented.

'I'll be out in a second. Go back an' lie down.'

'What's the matter?' asked Paul as he stood beside Conall's bed in a red-and-white-striped bathrobe and flip-flops.

'Feelin rotten. Must be malaria. I'm sick to my stomach an' so weak I can hardly live.'

'Probably malaria all right. We'll get you to the hospital at Longoma in the morning an' see what can be done.' Whenever

HEART IN HAND

anyone felt queasy, Paul supposed it was a touch of malaria, and he was generally right.

The hospital in Longoma was a rural hospital with a small staff. Safely delivering babies and curing children of diarrhoea with Dioralyte were its strong points. And the staff could relieve sufferers of a troublesome appendix. However, the place did not have any great 'diagnostic possibilities', as one of the doctors put it. They too supposed Conall's complaint to be malaria and promptly dosed him with Fansidar.

'That's strong stuff,' said Paul, speaking from experience. 'Should get you back on your feet pretty quickly.'

Meanwhile word got round by bush telegraph that Conall was in hospital and Brother Robert arrived from the mission in Kalabushi and Sister Susan from Munsar. Together with Paul, they sat by his bed all that long day. Conall didn't seem to get any better. The dark circles forming round his eyes worried Sister Susan. She suggested that they take him up country to the hospital at Kameru, where they would be better able to determine what exactly was the matter.

The western sky, visible through the hospital window, had become a delicate crimson. As night quickly descended, it blushed more deeply and inky palm trees stood out starkly against it. Mean vultures, like dehydrated turkeys, skulked on the roof of the hospital, their claws scraping the zinc, setting teeth on edge. Out in the compound, chickens were beginning to roost in the mango trees to avoid the menace of nocturnal snakes.

A nurse came and administered a sedative so that Conall might have a comfortable night. 'Conall, it's time to be gettin back to base, but we'll be here first thing in the mornin,' said Paul. 'If necessary, we'll take you to Kameru, but with the help of God the Fansidar will have done its work by then an you'll be feelin better.'

'Thanks. Safe home. See you all in the mornin,' whispered Conall wearily. Night engulfed the purple wine on the horizon. A nurse lit a lamp and the twenty patients in Conall's ward settled down to sleep as best they could.

Conall slept fitfully. His head was pulsing with pain, his mouth was parched, the tongue feeling woollen and intrusive. He sipped a little water. The coolness of it brought him some relief. He dozed.

Next time he awoke, his head was still throbbing, and angry spasms were surging through his stomach. 'What if I should die?' The possibility struck him for the first time. Imagine dying in an obscure hospital in the depths of the African bush, all alone, far from Ireland, family and loved ones, without even the presence of his fellow missionaries to console him. So near and yet so far, he lamented. The very thought of going this way distressed him profoundly. At least he had God. But did he? 'My God, my God, why have you forsaken me?' In his sudden desolation he empathised with the anguished words of the dying Christ and in his clouding mind began to hold on by his fingernails to hope and trust. His fraying thoughts hovered over his native Cliffs of Moher, the wind blew fresh on his burning face, the seagulls, no bigger than butterflies, flitted far below on the sheer sides of those vast monuments of nature. The crashing sea was no more than just a distant sigh. He saw the family home and farm nestling at the feet of the powdery blue Burren Mountains. Had his brother, Eanna, and sister, Roisin, returned from a musical seisiún in a Doolin pub? And were Mam and Dad still up to share that intimate late night cup of tea with them? Ah, those never-to-be-forgotten moments, when one was treasured so deeply.

Despite his acute discomfort, he was drifting again. In the twilight zone between wakefulness and sleep, stimulating, insightful thoughts seemed to form in his mind, but when he sought to grasp them and relate them to reality, they eluded him. Where did such thoughts come from? Into what world did they vanish? So relevant, yet so intangible. 'O God, don't let me die alone like this,' he pleaded, and mercifully faded into oblivion.

A pounding in his head awoke him. The parched tongue seemed to fill his whole mouth, which made breathing awkward. He wanted to reach for the glass of water. His hand would not obey his head. The severest spasms, yet, racked his stomach. Again there was the violent shaking and a terrifying tingling in the extremities as though life were ebbing away. On closing his eyes he had the dizzying sensation of sinking, sinking, sinking into some great void. Good God! Mother Mary! This was it. He was slipping away without a soul by his side. Without knowing whether his voice sounded or not, he cried out, 'Nurse!'

A young nurse with a fine African face was at his side. He strove to talk to her. She quickly summoned a second nurse to go get a doctor. Then she leaned her ear to his mouth and stroked his feverish brow. 'Could you please hold my hand, nurse?' She gently took his hand in hers and sat by his side. 'What is your name?'

'Precious,' she replied.

A faint smile passed over the pale boyish face, topped by wavy auburn hair. Dreamily, as he gazed, the delicate bronze hand of the girl transformed itself into his mother's care-worn hand, his father's firm grasp, the hand of Eanna, the hand of Roisin, the hand of every human being in the world. Last of all it became a fine-wrought hand that bore the jagged wound of a cruel nail. Then what seemed soft raindrops moistened his skin, and the hand in his pressed gently and withdrew. Suddenly he was in a great tunnel of light. He started walking into the light ... Hesitating for a moment, he looked fondly back. Thousands of hands were outstretched to him in farewell. Once more he resolutely faced the brightness. To his delight, there were myriad hands, suffused in light, stretched out to him in welcome. Towards these he now strode purposefully and looked back no more.

Precious wiped a tear from her eye, and covered the pale but still faintly smiling face with a sheet. The doctor rushed in. 'Too late, doctor,' she said with a forced professional crispness. 'It's all over.'

'More serious than we thought,' mused the doctor. 'Had to be typhus.'

'Or blackwater fever.'

The doctor pulled down the sheet and looked at the body. 'It was typhus all right.' Telltale purple spots had appeared. He covered the prostrate figure once more.

***

In a farmhouse nestling beneath the Burren Mountains, Mrs Eileen McEvoy was dreaming. In her dream she was standing, as she had often done, awaiting the arrival of Conall, Eanna, and

Roisin from school. The pathway to her door led over a grassy knoll at some distance. Any moment now the three heads would appear. It was one of those cloudless days when the drowsy blue of the sky seemed even to tinge the green of the earth. A lark soared, immersed in a rippling pool of song. To her amazement only Conall came over the grassy knoll and he was a fully grown young man. He approached with that captivating smile of his, holding out both hands to her. She grasped them firmly, and they gazed into each other's eyes. The smile faded from the face of Conall and he seemed sad. Then little by little he withdrew his hands from hers. She gasped and clung on all the more. A brief shadow of pain swept across his countenance. And despite her efforts to hold on, he slipped away inexorably.

She awoke abruptly filled with unease. Thank God it was all only a dream. She was safe in her bed and Conall on his African mission. But try as she might, there was no shaking off the sense of foreboding. She awoke her husband, Sean.

'What's wrong?' he asked sleepily.

She graphically related the whole dream. 'I'm awful worried about Conall.'

'For God's sake, woman, will you have sense. 'Twas only a dream. An' not a word of this to Eanna and Roisin. It'll only upset them for no reason. They're cracked about Conall.'

The cock crew loudly out in the barn and wan daylight peered in through the windows. In the semi-darkness the dawn chorus was already in full throat. At that moment in faraway Longoma, as though through some cosmic imperative, thousands of chirping crickets fell abruptly silent and, as if holding their breaths, listened. The silence was as sudden as the muezzin terminating the phrases of his early morning Arabic chant in the tower of the ghostly white village mosque

Sean got up and commenced to dress.

'What are ye doin?'

'I might as well get up an' milk the cows.'

'It's too early.'

'A fat chance I have now of goin back to sleep.' As he went towards the cowhouse, he paused and looked towards the grassy knoll. For thirty years he had worked this farm in cold and heat, driven by a love for Eileen and the children. Six unending years they had awaited for the arrival of Conall, who came like manna in the desert. He was then quickly followed by Eanna and Roisin. 'The Lord has given an' the Lord has taken away. Blessed be – What am I sayin?' he checked himself and shuddered. It was just that experience would not let him dismiss Eileen's intuitions and dreams lightly. Sadness settled on him like a cold mist that seeps into the core of one's being.

Eanna and Roisin had the usual rushed breakfast, kissed their mother, and called 'so long' to their father down in the farmyard. Roisin said that that very day she'd be sending an early birthday card to Conall to make sure that it would get to Africa on time.

'Dammit, that reminds me,' said Eanna. 'I should do the same.'

'Sean, come up for your breakfast. It's been a long mornin and you must be famished, you crathur,' cried Eileen.

As Sean was topping his egg, Shep, Conall's dog, charged towards the grassy knoll. Eyes wide, they waited. Over the crest appeared – the telegram boy. Exchanging a look of terror, Sean and Eileen searched for each other's hand.

It's the Tears of Things

'Let's go and pay our respects to Chief Shumbapano,' said Fr Guiseppe to his visitor, Fr Luke.

'Good idea.'

There wasn't even a hint of darkness in the sunny sky as they set out into the bush. The dirt road sliced its way through deep teak forests for many a mile. At last they came to a clearing and found their way impeded by a crude wooden gate. It was the entry into Chief Shumbapano's compound. They waited to be acknowledged. A well-built young guard eventually approached the gate. He wore a khaki uniform with striking red epaulets while, perched on his head, was a wide-rimmed bush hat with an Australian tilt over the left ear.

'Who are you?' the guard inquired.

'The *mupadire* from St Kizito's Mission and a visiting friend.'

'And your business?'

'We'd like to pay our respects to the chief.'

He lumbered off to consult with his patron. Luke queried the name Shumbapano, which, according to Guiseppe, meant 'there be lions hereabouts', and looking at the faded gold of the vast bush and the profusion of dark acacia trees spreading their thorny umbrellas, he could well believe it. Guiseppe said that the name wasn't to be found in the local language and must have been borrowed from a neighbouring people. He couldn't remember who told him its meaning. After some minutes there was a noisy scurrying of chickens, the cries of women and furiously barking dogs that ran to the gate with paradoxically wagging tails. The retainer came back, swung wide the gate, and the wives of the chief and their children sallied out to welcome the missionaries.

'*Mutende mwane*', they said as they clapped their hands once, placed the right hand over the heart, clapped hands once more and extended the right hand in greeting. '*Mutende mwane*', the visitors replied and went through the same little ritual.

IT'S THE TEARS OF THINGS

'The chief will see you,' said the guard and indicated a hillock topped by a thatched rondavel where Shumbapano sat profiled in regal isolation.

The men climbed the hillock. *'Mutende mwane,'* said the chief, clapping his hands once, placing the right hand over his heart, clapping his hands once more, and then extending the right hand for them to shake. The handshake was probably an adaptation to the white man. He was tall, strong and of noble bearing. All sat in silence. The other side of the hillock revealed a brooding River Lunga, deep and sinister, snaking its way to the far Zambezi. By now the sky had darkened over.

After a time Shumbapano spoke softly and had a lengthy conversation in the local language with Fr Guiseppe. Luke, the visitor, couldn't follow, but noticed that they kept on glancing at the crawling Lunga. The chief pointed to a particularly dark spot just below the hillock, where there was a bend in the river.

'The chief is very sad,' announced Guiseppe at length.

'I'm so sorry.'

'His eldest son, Musonga, was taken by a crocodile in that spot he indicated, three weeks ago.'

Luke looked at Shumbapano. A hand brushed over his face and downcast eyes in a typical African gesture. Luke often tried to interpret that gesture. In this case could it be a quiet shielding of a private grief and broken heart? Or could it be a question of fending off misfortune?

'Musonga went for a swim with a younger brother,' Guiseppe continued. 'He undressed and jumped in. Almost immediately he was dragged underneath the water. The brother waited apprehensively. Musonga appeared above the water. He rubbed his eyes in which there was a look of raw terror. Then he was jerked underneath once more and disappeared, forever. Startled by the shrieks of the younger brother the whole family rushed down to the river. On the bank there was a shirt, on the water some blood. There was nothing to do.'

All sat in profound silence. Down in the compound a chicken squawked jarringly. Finally the chief seemed to overcome his great internal distress and addressed Fr Luke courteously. The chief would like to know your business, Guiseppe interpreted.

'Sir,' said Luke somewhat apologetically, 'I am sharing on the subject of small Christian communities.'

'I am not a Christian myself, but I know it is an important subject.'

'Indeed.'

'And how is your mission progressing?'

'Slowly, I'm afraid, sir. Very slowly.'

Shumbapano paused. 'My people have a proverb that says, When God cooks, there is no smoke.'

The saying utterly intrigued Luke and left him with 'long long thoughts'.

One of the wives climbed the hillock and graciously presented the visitors with the gift of a chicken. That explains the squawk, thought Luke.

Before leaving, the missionaries took a family photograph. For this the chief donned his special garment, a somewhat incongruous black and deep-blue academic robe and on his head he wore a crown of ivory. Luke felt that in years to come this photograph would baffle descendants as to whether it represented a graduation or a coronation.

***

'A moving experience,' said Luke as he and Guiseppe drove away in the jeep. 'And what a dignified and wise man. It's really sad about the lad, but there's nothing to do. Time will have to take care of the hurt.'

'Nothing to be done,' said Guiseppe. 'If only that were true.'

'Meaning?'

'It's a never-ending nightmare. The African sees that everything which happens in life has a cause. An animal coughs up its heart's blood because a hunter spears it; the rain falls and the sun shines and, as a result, the crops thrive; a man and a woman make love and a child is born. Death too must have a cause, an explanation. The alternative is too bitter to contemplate: that he is at the mercy of blind forces that he can neither understand nor control. There is no such thing as chance in the traditional African world.'

'So what about death? What is the explanation?'

'Let me tell you a little story. For years a wretched man with ragged clothes, matted hair and bloodshot eyes used to come to St Kizito's for help. It so happened that there was once an epidemic of diphtheria in his native village and a witch-finder was brought in to divine the cause. In a dark hut, lit by the leaping flames of fire, he scattered his little bag of bones, consulted the auguries, and eventually declared the man in question a witch and the source of all the villagers' sorrow. That man was summarily driven from the village and from that day on was an outcast.'

'Appalling!' cried Luke.

'Well, people struggle as best they can to cope with the mysteries of life. But sure enough that man's existence was sad, sad. And when he died alone on a forest path, no one would touch the body. An unspeakable tragedy for an African, because he believes that his spirit cannot rest unless he is properly buried. So the hapless man would be a nameless wanderer throughout eternity as he had been in time.'

'And the Christians?'

'It's odd that you should say that,' Guiseppe continued. 'At this very moment I am refusing to celebrate the eucharist with one community that has driven out a poor widow, accusing her of being a witch. AIDS is doing the damage this time. I'm trying to shock them into reflecting on the gravity of the situation. But it's all so complicated. You see, you may know something with your mind, but if it doesn't register in the gut, it's useless. An irrational fear takes over. In my experience fear prevails with many people. Man, the same is true of ourselves. Go to a hotel and look for Room 13. You'll not find it. Incidentally, I buried that man I was talking about myself.'

'Any repercussions?'

'No. No one will stop you, if you're mad enough to do it. And it could be that there is a gnawing doubt in the minds of people about the validity of their superstitious practice anyway.'

'So, Guiseppe, it wasn't the crocodile that killed Musonga?'

'No. It was only the instrument. Besides, they say that some people turn themselves into crocodiles to achieve their sinister purposes.'

'The story of Musonga goes on then?'

'Unfortunately ... never endingly,' Guiseppe sighed and fell silent.

Luke too got lost in his own thoughts. Shumbapano came to mind. When God cooks, there is no smoke. Brilliant. Yet for all his great wisdom, the chief could not unloose the tyrannical grip of a fierce logic and dark forces whose origins were lost in the mists of pre-history. Such was the great tapestry of life; a paradoxical weaving of wisdom and ignorance, light and darkness, kindness and unwitting cruelty. The fabric could benefit from a cleansing in the blood of Christ. The beast that waited for Musonga in the dark waters of the Lunga was still at large in the world and would go on insatiably consuming humans until someone could break the fated sequence.

The atmosphere had turned oppressive. Luke's eyes drooped and his chin sank on his chest. Then it happened. He was transported into a surreal world of swirling vapours. And there she was, immersed in those vapours, a little girl who had been in the photograph taken at the compound. She had caught his eye then and she did so now, the delicately rounded face, doe-like eyes and captivating smile.

But what was this almost imperceptibly approaching through the mists? He peered and peered, yet could only discern a formless mass. As though time suddenly telescoped, the girl was transformed into the beautiful, gazelle-like woman she promised to become. But, my God, thought Luke with consternation, there she is standing, oblivious and vulnerable, directly in the path of the coming phantom.

For an age he waited helplessly for the obscure mass to take shape. When it did so, he was numbed with horror. It looked as though he was being called to witness the wheel of retribution come full circle from that tragic day on the Lunga as a great reptile bore down stealthily but inexorably on that lovely creature. *No!*

'You all right?' It was Guiseppe.

'Sorry, just a bad dream.' And a shudder swept through his whole frame.

Then there was a flash of lightening and a distant roll of thunder. Luke wondered if he hadn't been awakened by the thunder. A few raindrops like stray tears streamed down the windscreen. The rains were late this year.

An Unfortunate Error

On 6 September 1968 Swaziland gained its independence from Britain amid joyous celebrations. Princess Alexandra of Kent, accompanied by her husband, Angus Ogilvie, represented Queen Elizabeth for the historic transfer of power. And on behalf of Swaziland, King Sobhusa II was present in the Somhlolo Stadium, Lobamba, venue for the ceremony, in all the feathered splendour and russet sarong-like glory of his native costume. What I remember most of all was the march past of the Swazi regiments, brandishing knobkerries, spears and black-and-white patterned, animal-skin shields. These regiments were headed by the Salesian High School Band playing stirring tunes, among them 'Onward Christian Soldiers'. I thought there was something of a culture clash there, for many of the warriors would have been of native African religion, heavily into a cult of ancestors. The thousands of impis themselves sang those haunting Zulu chants – swelling and fading – that so impressed in the eponymous film. As well as the school band, that of the Malawi Rifles was on hand for the occasion in light khaki uniforms complete with flat-topped, conical red fezes with tassels. 'Upturned flower-pots', a nearby lady dubbed them.

As part of the celebrations, there was also an exhibition for some days in the Manzini Fair Ground. I was particularly struck by the native Sibhaca dancing. This was a quite unique type of line dancing done by men to the accompaniment of much drumming, whistling and vigorous stomping of feet in unison. In fact the stomping of feet was so strenuous that I feared there would be sprained ankles. And the dust raised! They performed with bare torsos, but with loin-skins fashioned from leopard hides and royal red feathers stuck in their abundant hair. On their feet they wore hairy animal anklets that shook with, and seemed to emphasise, the power of the stomping. At certain points in the routine the audience cooed their appreciation; why, I didn't know, but I sup-

AN UNFORTUNATE ERROR

posed they saw finer points that I was not aware of. There was laughter too because the routines were related to historical and topical happenings and, no doubt, had satirical content.

An added attraction at the show was a parade of floats. These featured commercial themes for the most part. There was, however, one belonging to some Christian group that caught the attention. First of all, it featured a friend of mine Dorothy, who in her little canoe was rowing furiously on a dark tumultuous sea of static turmoil. She was headed towards a flashing lighthouse in a desperate attempt to reach salvation. Despite her monumental efforts she was, of course, making no progress. Though seemingly about to be swallowed beneath the waves, she took a moment out from her fraught situation to wave and smile at friends in the crowd. 'Good girl, Dot,' they roared. 'Keep it up. You'll make it!' The reader will be relieved to hear she did, because I saw her having tea and cucumber sandwiches in the hospitality tent afterwards.

On the occasion of Independence, foreign nations were striving to curry favour with the newborn nation. The American stand, for example, displayed an amazing piece of moon rock. That, surely, would take some beating. In these high stakes, the British pulled a master stroke. Every so often, they distributed armfuls of attractive textile bags that became much sought after. The result was that crowds of Swazis were always milling around the British stand in an effort to get them. A colourful Union Jack was emblazoned on these bags; the result was that Swaziland was flooded with Union Jacks for months, probably years, afterwards. What a simply achieved, inexpensive, political and diplomatic triumph. The competing nations could only groan.

The seasons came and went and 1968 is now a long time ago. Yet before that first Independence Day becomes an irrevocable part of 'yesterday's one thousand years', I must recall the first anniversary. There was a feeling in the nation that facing the challenge of independence, there wasn't enough enthusiasm in the populace. 'Umph' was in fact the word used. This certainly was the sentiment of the *Times of Swaziland*, which in bold capitals about two inches high on its front page urged: SWAZILANDERS ARISE! The only problem was that they omitted the 'i' in arise.

Oops! Funny how we humans are careful in dealing with minor errors while huge ones escape us. The unfortunate misprint kept the Swazis, who have a wonderful sense of humour, laughing for a long time – which wasn't a bad outcome either.

The Cotton Tree

The Cotton Tree extended her arms in the morning sun. A herd of staccato-bleating goats were driven by to pastures; occasionally one or other of them would skip suddenly in a brief outburst of erotic energy. How much more alert were they than the sheep, mused the Cotton Tree. At the approach of a vehicle they would bound off, white tails aloft, into the safety of the bush, whereas the sheep would wander aimlessly about the road, inviting death.

Some villagers went silently to their fields; sinewy men with hoes and machetes flashing; regal women with large baskets upon their heads. Others were spreading out rice for drying on the scrupulously brushed surfaces in front of their huts.

Children were on their way to the mission school, Africans incongruously dressed in their uniforms, costumed to play the European part.

On the surrounding roofs vultures skulked like under-nourished turkeys, as white-collared crows, popularly known as 'minister' birds, fussed about them with mincing steps, claws scratching on corrugated iron, setting teeth on edge.

Smaller birds chattered and chirped in the Cotton Tree herself. And a hornbill flew past complaining bitterly.

As generation after generation washed over the village these were typical sights and sounds. Of course the motor car had come and scattered red dust on the vivid green of the bush, but the leaves of the Cotton Tree soared far beyond its reach to create a delicate embroidery against the sun-suffused blue of the sky.

The Cotton Tree gave ample shade to women in vibrant long skirts and matching headscarves, who sold peeled oranges to parched travellers, while their tots nestled in the nooks at her base.

The Cotton Tree was a rallying point in joy and in sorrow, at life's greater moments and seemingly lesser moments which are, nevertheless, often indelibly impressed on the memory and recalled with nostalgia. Mothers presented their newborn babes to the village there. Trembling on the verge of vigorous adolescence, young initiates walked sprightly past, the girls with blanched faces and the boys with shaven heads. These the Cotton Tree followed through all the years until they crawled towards death in revered and desiccated old age.

And the lesser moments. When the paramount chief's horn sounded, hoarse and cacophonous, people gathered there to sort out the ordinary affairs of the chiefdom; the court too met in her shelter to resolve the minor squabbles that arose – mammy palaver and petty thefts.

A delightful informality reigned in the court. On one occasion an allegation was being made, but it's origin was uncertain. 'Who is making this allegation anyway?' demanded the frustrated judge. The local eccentric Fatmata (a corruption of 'Fatima', the name of the Prophet Mohammed's daughter) immediately shot up and declared, 'Your Honour I am the alligator!' The whole assembly just fell apart.

White men always caused a stir with their strange ways. Like that bejeaned young fellow with unkempt yellow hair and transparent ears who stood, transfixed, looking up at the Cotton Tree one day, saying something about his never expecting to see a poem as lovely as a tree and how no one could make a tree save God. Such a rigmarole to end up saying something so obvious.

And so the Cotton Tree had been at the heart of village life as day endlessly ebbed into day: sparkling mornings, burning afternoons, tangible sunsets that enveloped one in a roseate haze, and nights filled with the drilling of crickets and the croaking of frogs. It seemed it would continue thus for all eternity.

But eternity is a long time. Change, alas, did come to the village, and the morning mist dripping from the branches of the Cotton Tree became tears of sorrow.

It all started with a bizarre chain of events. A bridge collapsed and, amid scenes of agony, nine dead were brought back to the village; two more were killed off a motor cycle; then there was the appalling murder and robbery of a gentle Syrian; and, finally, three sets of twins were born, which certainly boded ill for the hamlet.

THE COTTON TREE

Worst of all people started shunning the Cotton Tree. From a distance there were furtive glances in her direction; some even turned their faces away. If a child strayed towards her, it was followed by the shrill voice of her mother fearfully calling it back. Juju men went about with cupped hands whispering into inclined ears.

Then one day she (at last!) joyously saw three strong men, returning from the fields with shining machetes, coming to rest in her shade. It was Momoh, Dura and Abu, all of whom she had loved since childhood. As they drew near the joy turned to apprehension; their eyes were sullen, their faces grave. Then terror. The machetes were axes.

Without even pausing, they started hacking at her unresisting flesh. Why should she resist? Had she not harboured a secret hope that in death she might become one of those long-boats which ferried her children across the great river that she could spy from her topmost branches? Her lifeblood began to ooze. As shock after shock of the cruel axes reverberated through her limbs, birds fled the branches to the seeming security of the surrounding bush.

A mighty groan shook the village. The inhabitants lurked in dark corners with downcast eyes. There was a screaming of birds scattering in horror from the falling giant which crashed to earth with an awesome roar and devastated the surrounding vegetation. Not all of the birds were lucky. A weaver-bird, pinned by a branch, fluttered vainly for a moment, but then the eyes glazed over, the head swivelled limp and the creature, wings still outstretched, lay motionless.

As the world held its breath, Momoh said, 'Who would ever have thought that our old friend the Cotton Tree would betray us. That she would give a home in her branches to those witches who killed our brothers and sisters. And cursed us with twins.'

'Who would ever have thought it,' chorused Dura and Abu.

And the dust settled on the miracle that had been three hundred years a-growing, yet was brought low in one short afternoon.

And a hornbill flew past complaining bitterly.

Shark

Would I or would I not go for a swim? The sky over Gordon's Bay was an agitated cauldron of swirling dark clouds. The ocean, which should have presented a smoother face because it was high summer, was choppy and foam-flecked. After a string of sunny days, this one was chilly, but as I dipped a tentative toe in the bay, I realised that it would be warmer in the water than out. So I took the fateful plunge and was soon battling sizeable waves as I swam out to sea.

Seabirds wailed overhead as they were tossed about by the wind. My eyes smarted from the salt water and I retched as I swallowed some. However, swimming in the turbulent ocean was exhilarating. Then suddenly I spotted it – the dorsal fin of a shark, about twenty yards away. Almost immediately it disappeared behind the swell of a wave.

Crisis. To this day I bear the scars.

The appearance of a shark was totally unanticipated. One simply did not expect to find sharks around the Cape of Good Hope, where the cold fingers of the Atlantic reach deeply into the Indian Ocean. However, when all was said and done, there was nothing to stop a determined shark from going wherever it wished.

Though my blood ran cold, some relevant facts about sharks flashed through my mind. They are guided not so much by sight as by vibrations, so I must not thrash about in the water. I had to remain as motionless as I could. I glanced at the distant shore. No hope of attaining it. Sharks can spurt up to forty kilometres per hour.

'Madam, if that kid should fall in, a shark is going to get to him much faster than I can.' The reproving voice of the attendant at a seaquarium, speaking to a lady who sat her little boy on the edge of a shark tank for a better look, came to me from down the years.

If sharks have already eaten, they aren't greedy. There was hope there. I gently turned over on my back and did what as boys we called 'the deadman's float'. An ironic term in the event.

Then I simply waited – breathlessly. A complex, rational entity reduced to nothing more than a helplessly floating human bait. 'Angry fish,' I once heard a weathered, whipcord old man of the sea cry out to some unsuspecting swimmer as he sighted a shark on the horizon off the coast of Manabi in Ecuador. The 'angry' fish silently gliding somewhere near could now eat me with as little compunction as I might eat a shrimp. A situation like the one in which I found myself concentrates the mind wonderfully. And the fundamental question, demanding a rapid response, forced itself upon me as indeed it must, in some shape or form, on anyone in similarly drastic circumstances.

The trauma can only have lasted a few minutes, yet it felt like an age. Totally abandoned to the will of the sea, I was thrown up and cast down by the heaving waves. Then, of a sudden, there it was again. Right beside me. The dorsal fin. But before my terrified eyes it miraculously transformed itself into a bird and flew away.

There are seabirds without feathers on the neck that can, at certain angles, look exactly like the dorsal fin of a shark.

It is impossible to describe the overwhelming relief I felt at that moment. Even now, years later, the mere memory of the event can send shivers down my spine, and I will bear the psychic scars of the encounter till my dying day. So much for sharks.

Good News

A young Masai lad called Lemalian, was out with his father, seeking good grazing for their cattle. Suddenly, something lying by the wayside caught the attention of the father. He stopped and picked it up. It was a tibia bone. 'Do you know what this is?' he asked his son.

The lad didn't.

'Well, it is a bone belonging to your grandfather.'

They both observed it for a while and then the father tossed it by the wayside once more and they went on tending their cattle.

The Masai believe in God (*Enkai*) and point to the highest point in the heavens as his dwelling place. In former times God lived much nearer to them – just overhead in fact. But a foolish clan among the tribe fired arrows in that direction and God indignantly ascended to the most distant point in the sky. The clan responsible live with the opprobrium to this day.

Although the Masai believe in God, they do not believe in an afterlife, which is rather incongruous. Indeed they have no future tense in their language. For this reason they do not treat human remains with awe. Traditionally, when a member of the tribe dies, they are put out in the bush to be devoured by wild animals. This is why the father was able to come by the tibia of Lemalian's grandfather and it was also the reason why he casually threw it to one side once he had shown it to his son. But the occasion remained as a depressing memory in the mind of Lemalian.

Some years later the boy out of curiosity accompanied a friend to a religious gathering. It so happened that it was Easter Sunday and the people were joyfully celebrating the feast. In his homily the priest talked about someone called Jesus, who was the Son of God. He told his listeners about how he was crucified, died and rose from the dead to save all of us. And he went on to say that just as Jesus had risen from the dead, we too would be raised up to be happy with him forever in a place called heaven. Lemalian was astonished. He thought back to the tibia bone incident. A huge burden was removed from his heart. This was indeed good news.

Lemalian embraced those good tidings with all his heart and today he is a priest, appropriately named Peter – after *Petrus* the rock – and is bringing that heart-warming news to all of his people. With great difficulty he located the tibia of his grandfather, now overgrown with scrub, and gave it decent burial.

Saving the Fish from Drowning
(Traditional African story heard in Tanzania)

Long, long ago in our land there was a rainy season such as had never been seen before, or since, for that matter. The water was everywhere and the animals were running up the hills to escape it. So fast did the floods come that many of them drowned, except for the monkeys, who smartly climbed to the treetops to avoid the rising water. From their vantage point they looked down on the raging waters and to their consternation saw the fish swimming and jumping about in the flood. The creatures seemed to be enjoying themselves yet it had to be a false impression, the monkeys concluded. In reality those unfortunate souls were in a dangerous situation. One of the monkeys called out to a companion, 'Look down, my friend, at these poor creatures. They are going to drown. Do you see how they are fighting for their lives?'

'Yes, indeed,' replied the other monkey.

'What a shame! It is impossible for them to escape to the hills because they don't seem to have any legs. But what can we do to save them?'

'Let me see. If we wade in at the edge of the flood, where the waters aren't deep enough to cover us, maybe we can help them to get out.'

So all the monkeys did just that. With much difficulty they caught the fish one by one and placed them on dry land. After a time, there was a great pile of them lying on the grass – all of them motionless.

'Do you see how tired these creatures are?' asked one of the monkeys. 'They are just sleeping and resting now. Had it not been for us, my friends, all these poor creatures without legs would have drowned.'

'Yes,' observed another, 'they were trying to escape us because they couldn't understand our good intentions but, when they wake up, they will be very grateful because we have brought them salvation.'

Christopher, I Owe You

People are often disappointed when their efforts are not rewarded with immediate results. I recall an occasion in Ghana when, as usual, I had been sharing with a group on the subject of initiating small communities. The discussion was difficult. Lots of roadblocks. When it was all over, I must have looked somewhat bedraggled, even dispirited, because a man called Christopher approached and told me the following story.

'James, I am an agricultural instructor and my work is to help the farmers in the locality. Twenty years ago, hoes were the only tools used for cultivation around here. In the cause of progress we decided to get the farmers using oxen instead for ploughing, so we decided to provide a team of oxen for every one of them. And you know what happened? They ate the oxen! But now twenty years later, I can tell you, James, that oxen are used for ploughing all over this area. And twenty years from now small communities that can link together for the betterment of people will have spread all over this area.'

It was soon twenty years later, and Christopher was right.

Obviously what he was telling me was that, though his solution to the sole use of hoes was actually eaten, he did not throw his hands up in despair, but set about slowly changing the minds and customs of people. In other words he grasped that there was a *process* involved. Something that had gone on for centuries could not be changed overnight; from hoe to plough was a considerable technological leap. No doubt there were many more lapses and disappointments along the road before the new method was fully accepted. Even a few more juicy sirloin steaks may have been thoughtlessly consumed.

Many things happened to me and many things were said during long years of travel and work. Only some of them have stayed in my mind. Perhaps they were the events and words that most deeply impressed me. I have never forgotten the prophetic

Christopher, a slight man with a narrow face, greying hair and dark intelligent eyes. He clearly brought home to me the utter importance of having a sense of process – far from being the only or most profound lesson of the occasion, as I'm sure you'll agree. And he also gave my wavering spirits such a lift that I can feel the exhilaration to this day. Thanks Christopher, I owe you.

Land of Neutral Faces

The tropical downpour ceased, the sky brightened somewhat and its light gleamed on the dampness of the broad banana leaves. The branches of palm, paw-paw and cacao hung limp after the deluge as the steaming bush extended in all directions like a vast green sea.

In the midst of the sea, there was the school. An aerial view would reveal a grassy compound fringed with red-roofed buildings. On three sides, beneath the eaves of the buildings, there were obvious classrooms opening on to corridors with arching cream colonnades, and to the east assorted residences and offices. Some sisters, garbed in blue and white, were cultivating vegetables near one of the residences. The arches and undulating russet tiles bore an unmistakable Hispanic stamp.

A closer look at the school took away its colonial sheen. Broken windows, flaking paint, non-functioning toilets and wild unkempt grass spoke of years of neglect. To one side there was a rusting vehicle being slowly engulfed by the tentacles of a luxuriant creeper.

In the compound, a long-tailed widow-bird was performing an aerial mating dance above a seemingly unimpressed, diminutive mate that flitted coyly from one yielding grass stem to another. The red-and-yellow weavers too had boldly hung their nests on the protective window bars of the school and, perched beside them, were trilling ecstatically with quivering wings.

People were beginning to assemble. Little knots of boys and girls stood about in conversation. At a distance from the students, the teachers too were chatting away. To one side some boys were tentatively kicking a plastic football about. Serious combat would have to await the midday break.

A porter with gaunt face and grizzled hair sat by the entrance as the students streamed through. His eyes were large and considerate. Every now and then a slap rang out as he dealt himself a blow on the cheek or arm. Those cabouri flies! In Gabon there were only the mosquitoes that attacked by night. Bad enough. But here there were also these damned cabouris that came in swarms and devoured you in broad daylight.

Isolated on one corner of the compound there was a guard in green fatigues, a gun slung about his neck. His bulbous eyes roved lasciviously over the girls from an over-fed face and his stomach billowed over his military belt in a most unmilitary fashion.

A bell tinkled and all the students formed into lines according to their classes. Before them stood an imposing headmaster in a safari suit. Then came the sound of eggs frying from a loudspeaker hung on a nearby column, followed by the first tinny notes of the national anthem, formerly *God Save Azalia*, now *Micenius Save Azalia*: Micenius being the local dictator who had made God redundant. The guard's finger itched near the trigger of his gun.

'*Attention!*' roared the head. Students and teachers stiffened. In fact everyone in the compound froze: a cleaner stopped motionless with broom poised, a casual passer-by stood to attention facing the acacia tree where he had been relieving himself, and the cabouris descended unimpeded upon the hapless porter. The students commenced to sing with neutral faces as the guard eyed them wickedly.

The anthem finished, the classes peeled off in silence to walk along the corridors to their respective classrooms. Suddenly above the shuffling of feet there was the shrill whistling of a bird from the sisters' residence. It was Arturo, the convent parrot, lustily whistling the national anthem. The first form students tittered audibly. A shot rang out that shattered the plaster above their heads. Fearful white of eye glinted in dark faces and they fell silent. They were learning.

From dint of hearing the national anthem day in day out, Arturo had become quite proficient at whistling it. Such indeed was the repetition that even the scavenging crows could have attempted a fair rendition, let alone a sharp-eared parrot.

The guard slouched out of the compound. Everyone noticed, yet nobody looked. An hour later, there was the quiet hum of lessons in progress. Occasionally the shout of some frustrated teacher would ring out across the compound. But then the foreboding sound of an approaching jeep reduced all to an apprehensive quiet. It roared into the school and ploughed its way directly through the sodden earth to the sisters' house. With screeching brakes it slid to a halt. A captain and four soldiers jumped out.

Arturo sat on his perch, green feathers ending abruptly in a clownish red tail. He surveyed the intruders with what seemed a censorious, maiden aunt's eye, an aspect further suggested by the no-nonsense hooked beak, which gave the impression that he had just removed his spectacles.

The line of soldiers, rifles at the ready, dropped in front of the parrot on one knee.

'*Ready!*' yelled the captain.

Taking his cue from orders being barked, Arturo, with swelling breast, launched into a shrill rendering of – no atheist he – *God Save Azalia*.

'*Aim!*'

'*Fire!*'

Thus fell Arturo in a hail of bullets and flying feathers, gloriously whistling the national anthem.

Sister Prisca rushed belatedly on to the scene, her arms flailing. 'Animals!' she screamed, 'savages ... to call you animals and savages is to insult animals and savages.'

Sister Prisca was outspoken. A little heap of a nun with a furrowed, embattled face, Prisca must have been one of the few people in the world who had been thrown out of jail for being a nuisance. In or out of jail she could not be silenced. If eliminated, she would make a fearsome ancestor. This kept her from being killed.

The jeep refused to start. Three soldiers jumped out and pushed. It sprang to life and shot speedily away – leaving the cursing soldiers to find their own way back to barracks.

'Po' Arturo,' moaned Prisca, 'you so broken you no good eben fo' de soup.' With an upturned eye, Arturo regarded her with a fixed, surprised stare.

As the sound of the jeep died away and an awed silence descended on the compound, there came the distant whistling of a parrot. Yes, it was unmistakable – *God Save Azalia*. The departing soldiers spun round abruptly and peered into the depths of the bush.

Avonree Days

The Hedgehog

'I'm glad I'm with ye, Sean. I bumped into an ass here one night in the dark,' said Mickey. The air rang with unmalicious laughter.

The three pals were cycling home from the cinema and only Sean had a bicycle lamp. Mickey and Tommy rode somewhat to the rear.

'You're lucky you didn't bump into a garda,' replied Sean ... 'Will we go for a swim in the mornin?'

'Yeah, let's do that. The water should be nice,' answered Tommy.

It had been a good summer and, although it was late August, the warm weather continued.

Mickey demurred. 'I have to do messages.'

'We'll wait for ye,' said Tommy, 'Hey, is that a rabbit ahead of us?'

'It's a porcupine!' They braked.

'Solomon had a hundred wives and five hundred porcupines,' joked Sean. 'It says it in the Bible.' The others didn't see the joke.

Sean was a college boy. 'Philistines ... I'm wasting my sweetness on the desert air,' he complained. 'Anyway there aren't any porcupines in Ireland. Ye get them in Africa though ... very tasty, they say. This is a hedgehog.'

Now the lads had dismounted and were following the creature which ambled along in front of them, trapped by the light. It made as though to turn into the hedgerow. With a fateful boot Sean barred its way to freedom and urged it back on to the road. Terrified, the animal rolled itself into a tight protective ball. The boys nudged it with the toes of their shoes.

'Ouch!' cried Tommy who was wearing sandals. 'Its thorns prick.'

'Of course they prick, ye eejit,' mocked Sean. 'What did ye expect?'

Tommy fetched a hurley stick from the carrier of his bicycle and poked it with that. But the hedgehog adamantly refused to open.

'They say,' said Sean, 'that if a hedgehog rolls into a ball, the best way to get it to open up is to light a fire under it.'

'But that'd be cruel,' objected Mickey.

'Don't be an ass,' Sean replied. 'As soon as it feels the first little bit o' heat, it opens an' runs, so it does.'

Sean had matches, because he had begun to smoke – secretly for fear of his parents. 'Tommy, get some dried twigs an' bracken, an' we'll make a fire an' get this fella movin.'

Tommy hurried to the side of the road and groped for kindling with the help of the little light that reached him from the solitary lamp, which Sean steadily focused on the immobile hedgehog.

Mickey stood irresolute.

Soon the hedgehog was pushed on to a pile of dried grass, bracken and twigs. Sean struck a match and set the fire alight.

The flames soon leaped unexpectedly high. It had been a long dry summer. Sean and Tommy laughed with expectation as they waited for the hedgehog to uncurl quickly and trot away.

But the laughter soon turned to horror as it refused to do so. Indeed it gave a spasm and seemed to withdraw more tightly from the world. Quickly Sean grasped the hurley stick from Tommy and pushed the creature smoking and singed from the pyre. 'We need water or somethin,' said Sean indecisively.

Even while he was mumbling the words, Mickey was racing to a nearby stream. On reaching it he soaked his pullover in the cool water, rushed back and squeezed abundant rivulets all over the hapless creature. And he ran back and forth to the stream several times, repeating the process, until he eventually sank to his knees exhausted and wheezing. He was asthmatic.

'All right Mickey,' said Sean, getting a grip on himself, 'That'll be enough. He'll be fine now. We'll put him here in the ditch an' I bet you anything he'll be gone in the mornin'. I'll tell you what. We'll come at daybreak to see. Take my pullover an' put it on.'

After some restless hours they called for each other.

'Where are ye goin, Mickey?' his mother called out from upstairs. 'There's the messages to do.'

THE HEDGEHOG

'I'll be back in a minute, Mammy.'

'Ye better be. If you're not I'll malafooster ye.' She made her customary drastic if idle threat.

The boys cycled silently and tensely back to the scene. Day was edging in from the east and the birds were singing in the semi-dark. But the hedgehog hadn't moved. There it lay in its tight ball, charred and still.

They stood in silence for a long while, then turned away and commenced walking home sadly, pushing their bicycles alongside them.

'Why didn't he open?' asked Mickey at last.

'Why didn't he? The silly get,' replied Sean. 'It was all his own fault.'

'Yeah, all his own fault,' Tommy loudly agreed.

Mickey was not so sure and felt awful. He clung to the thought that the water might have eased the creature's pain, as he died.

Jerusalem, Jerusalem

Never will I forget the first time I saw the man whom in my mind I later came to know as Roll-on. Without legs, he sat in a crude wooden box with pram wheels attached, and propelled this vehicle along by means of a short baton in each hand.

His abnormality quickly attracted a gaggle of urchins, who began to taunt him in that cruel way which only thoughtless urchins can. Halting his box, he produced from beside him a short-handled pitchfork whose points glinted wickedly.

'Go home ye free-beef bastards!' he shouted over and over again at his tormentors, as he menacingly brandished his weapon. Obviously he did not appreciate this result, as he considered the gaggle, of De Valera's largess during the Economic War.

'There's nice language for ye,' said Mrs Murphy, who had come to her door to see what all the commotion was about. 'Does he have drink on him, I wonder?'

'Can't ye see he's legless?' retorted Paud Brennan, the town wag, with a twinkle in his eye.

The more Roll-on cursed, the more the children shrieked with glee.

Eventually Garda Mahoney arrived and ordered him to get a move on.

As a spectator, I watched the drama unfold from a distance. Now that it was seemingly over, I realised with a start that I would be late getting home with the milk. So I began walking briskly along the kerbstones at the edge of the footpath, imagining myself a balancing artist on the slack wire in Duffy's Circus. Maybe I was shaken by what I had seen because, inexplicably, I took a tumble. The milk can went flying up in the air and the liquid came splashing down all over me. Fearful of what would happen when I got home, I returned tearfully to the milkman, Tom Walsh, who refilled the vessel free of charge and restored my belief in humanity.

This contretemps distracted me a little from the Roll-on incident.

The following night I was seated at the fire with my mother and father. Being the oldest of the family on hand, I was allowed to sit by the warm glow of the turf and chat with them until it was time to make tea and go to bed. Jack, the greyhound, was stretched dozing at our feet dreaming his doggy dreams after a hearty feed of yellow meal.

Seemingly Roll-on had been the talk of the town that day. He had not moved along as the garda had ordered, but had returned to the streets of the town in the night.

'I believe the tongue of him was something awful,' said my mother.

'What happened to his legs?' I asked.

'Father Critchley had to get out of his bed an' shout from his upstairs window for him to stop his carry on.'

'What happened to his legs?' I persisted.

'At that,' continued mother imperviously, 'the men rushed out of Donovan's pub, snatched his pitchfork away from him, an' brought him down to the Great Bridge. They made as if they were going to throw him in for cursin an' carryin on under the priest's window. Then they ran him to the edge of the town an' told him he'd end up in the river for sure, if he dared show his face in the streets again. Jack McIntyre, the President of the Holy Family, gave him a mighty push down Daisy Hill, cryin out after the scurryin box, "roll on Rahilly!"'

"Ye hoor's ghosts!" the victim yelled back. "If only I had me legs, I'd show ye cowardly bastards ... like I showed Gerry at Wipers!"

'They say he lost his legs at the Somme, Tommy,' father at last answered my question.

'What's the Somme, Daddy?'

'A big battle in France during the Great War. Thousands and thousands were slaughtered in the mud there. An' the rats could talk to ye ... rats as big as cats. Your Uncle Tom was wounded at the Somme. His life was saved by a big brass medal of the Blessed Virgin that he wore on his chest. Ask him to show it to ye some time. He has it to this day. There's a great groove in it where it deflected a bullet.'

'What were they fightin for?'

'For the freedom of Ireland an' all small nations like it, son.'

'Although I was only a little girl,' said mother, 'I can remember the men all marchin off to war with the band playin and them in smart uniforms with shiny buttons.'

'Me too,' father added.

'And remember all the wives, black shawls on their heads, weepin? About a month after that, the first cheques arrived in the post office for them. When Mary MacLaverty came out and opened the cheque and saw the amount, she raised her eyes and arms to heaven cryin, "Jasus, if this be war, may there never be peace!"'

'Did Roll-on march out with those men?'

'Who's Roll-on?' she asked.

'The cripple ... Roll-on Rahilly.'

'I suppose he did, Tommy. Not from this town, but from some other one.'

'And was his wife delighted with the cheque?'

The mother gave him a long look. A curious child ... Yet maybe that was the reason.

'Did you hear what Paud Brennan had to say about this Roll-on?' father inquired.

'He said that a snail carries his house on his back, but he has it under his arse.' Father laughed uproariously. 'Under his arse,' he repeated. 'Wasn't that a good one? Under his arse.' And again he laughed heartily.

'Doesn't he have any home then?' I asked.

'The four sides of that box are the horizons of his world.'

Mother often surprised me by the things she said. They were like snatches from the poetry that we read at school.

My sleep is troubled in the night: huge rats crawling over dead soldiers; women wailing; Uncle Tom lying bleeding; Holy Mary, Mother of God, pray for us sinners, now ... if this be war ... trying to reach Uncle Tom, I stick helplessly in the mud ... may there never be peace ... can't move in the mud ... lifting feet but getting nowhere ... clouded angry faces, eyes dilated, teeth stripped ... roll on Rahilly ... no room here ... the freedom of small nations ... an ecstatic woman ... suddenly with flashing pitchfork Roll-on springs out of the dark– With a cry I bolt upright in my bed. My hair and face are damp with sweat. I consciously lie awake for a long time so as not to be sucked back into the miasma. Every little creak becomes a loud groan. Do I hear squeaking pram wheels on the road outside? I steal to the window. The night is impenetrable.

***

Only once more did I see Roll-on. It couldn't have been many years later.

Turning a corner, I come face to face with him in a narrow lane on the outskirts of our town. I stand paralysed by fear. With bated breath I almost feel the pitchfork sear my entrails. Eyes fixed straight ahead, however, he looks neither to left nor right, at me or anything else.

I'm told he went right through the town like that. A few early birds in Donovan's pub were awed at his passing. 'There's that fella that cursed and blasphemed round the street here a couple of years ago. 'So it is, the hoor.' 'Blaspheme did ye say? Sure didn't he even criticise the kindheartedness of our great leader, Mr De Valera.' The crippled man did not so much as glance their way. Neither did he lift his gaze to Fr Critchley's window. The few townspeople who were on the street at the time saw him, as did the ubiquitous Paud Brennan. But the witticisms withered within him. The Archconfraternity of the Holy Family was meeting that evening. From the church came the swelling voices, 'We stand for God and for his glory ... against his host we raise his standard ...' Roll-on slipped by in his box. The members of the Irish Transport and General Workers' Union, arraigned on the gospel side, were getting the better of ('Give it to the bastards!') the members of the British-influenced Trades Union Congress, drawn up on the epistle side.

***

Poor Roll-on. From time to time in life he comes back to haunt me from those ungentle days. Trapped in his box, he snarls defiantly at a hostile world, like a dog snarling futilely into the depths of space. As for my town, alas, it did not know the time of its visitation.

Interlude

The whole episode is indelibly fixed in my mind like the frame of a film that has been clicked to a halt for close scrutiny. Alongside me there is the ancient wall, lichen-studded and crowned with ivy, surrounding the site of a castle, long since gone. Donkeys and carts inch their way to the nearby creamery along the quiet village street, driven by farmers' boys wearing wellingtons with turned-down tops. The bright summer morning bounces off the windows, skylights and milk churns.

Particularly striking are the sparse clouds that hover on the horizon, largely because of their peculiar aspect. Silver and wispy, they have the whipped-up appearance of a distraught maniac's hair. Their static turmoil, so out of keeping with the tranquil morning, hints at distant disquiet.

As a fun-seeking nine-year-old, I am on my way for an early morning swim when, without the slightest warning, I am stuck to the ground by an immense realisation – eternity had no beginning. Of course I have heard this before. Often. But never has it registered like this. Eternity had no beginning. And eternity will have no end. Somehow I can cope with the fact of no end. Even myself I cannot see returning to an everlasting nothingness when at last they close my eyes with pennies and put me under the ground as they did recently with my beloved grandfather. But no beginning! The intellect speeds back through long eons and vast distances with the instantaneous rapidity of thought. Yet at the outmost reaches of reason, thought is abruptly arrested in flight by the windows of the mind that look out upon infinity and flounder to earth, stunned and helpless. And for all the long journey, it is as if I have never even started. Eternity had no beginning. Who made eternity?

I stand clasping my head in my hands. It feels as though it will shatter into a thousand pieces.

'You sir, are you in a trance or somethin?' It is the down to

INTERLUDE

earth voice of a farmer's boy making his exit from the creamery in his donkey and cart. I am blocking his path. I can't have been standing for long. A minute or two perhaps. However, it is one of those intrusions of eternity into time when the length of the interlude becomes quite irrelevant. To say that seconds become years and years seconds is helpful yet totally inadequate.

'You're lucky I'm not a motor car,' says the bemused farmer's boy.

Trying to picture this, I feel that on balance I am not as lucky as he.

Shaking the infinities from my brain, I remove my hands from my head and blink a few times. 'Sorry.' And I trot off in relief for a swim with Paddy Mackey in the Turning Hole.

The farmer's lad eyes me curiously as I go. He then shouts, 'Gee up, Neddy!' and gives his donkey a skelp across the buttocks with the reins.

The world is again in motion.

Dads' Army

September 3rd, 1939, will forever be remembered in Ballybeg for two reasons. On that day Kilkenny won the historic 'Thunder and Lightning' All Ireland Hurling Final by 'the usual one point', as the renowned Jack Lynch was to remark wryly, and World War II was declared in Europe. Joy was unbounded on winning the match, but the effects of the declaration of war were to be keenly felt later.

I have no recollection of our winning the game, but the effects of the war were to register with me fairly quickly. Rationing of such items as tea, sugar and butter soon became a reality and the tasty snow-white bread, made of wheat from the Canadian prairies, was to disappear. In its place we got the so-called black bread – a dirty off-white really – made from home-grown wheat. Although I was very young, I still had a memory of oranges and bananas, and missed them desperately – especially the bananas.

Heaven to me was a place where you could eat bananas all day. Later, I was to spend some years in Ecuador, one of the earth's greatest producers of bananas and was fed such a surfeit of them that I began to associate them with quite a different place – also beginning with 'h'.

But the most significant effect of the war was that De Valera declared Ireland would remain neutral in the European conflict. This did not please Churchill in the least because he would dearly have liked the use of Ireland's ports. There were even rumblings to the effect that they would be seized. This, coupled with the German menace, led to the 'Emergency' and the setting up of what largely appeared to me as a dads' army. I say this because all our fathers were in it, including my own. Younger men tended to join the regular army, Irish or British.

Very soon men in khaki uniforms, the Local Defence Force (LDF), began to appear on our streets, followed immediately by the Local Security Force (LSF), in navy blue outfits, and the Red Cross with white arm bands bearing striking red crosses. Even in the grim situation of glowering war clouds, people didn't lose their sense of humour. The LDF quickly became known as the Look, Duck and Fly brigade!

Military intimations continued. One night my father came home with a stout pair of combat boots. A new uniform soon followed. It was a light green like that of the regular army, with a newly designed, beret-like cap. And then came the rifles – this was serious stuff.

Truth to tell, the rifles looked ancient – throwbacks to World War I. What could you do with them against one of those German planes? Jack Delaney wanted to know.

'Ye see that big tree down there, Jack?' asked Tom Dooley.

'Yes.'

'Well, ye could be hidden in the branches and one of those planes could be flyin around and couldn't ye take it down with your rifle.'

'Sure there's no way ye could do that; he'd spot you immediately with them glasses they do be wearin and bomb ye.'

The next Sunday came and I saw some LDF men – my father among them – head off unexpectedly in the direction of Waterford in the back of a lorry. I wondered if Churchill had made good on his promise to seize the ports.

Things continued to hot up. One night there was a banging on Johnny Tynan's door. Johnny was a sterling member of the LSF – Ireland's answer to the Gestapo. His wife, Bridie, pulled up the window and stuck her head out and asked who was there.

The men below called out, 'Bridie, the Germans have landed up near Slievenamon. Tell Johnny he's to report to the barracks on the double.'

'Do ye want him to catch his death of cold?' asked Bridie and slammed the window closed. The fellows below had a good chuckle; as an exercise to test the alertness of the force, this was going badly.

War fever also invaded the classroom in the local primary school where Sister Clare was preparing a group of us for our First Holy Communion. Having produced a pot of home-made jam and two loaves of bread from her ample skirts, and fed us all, she was prodding us for information regarding hostilities. Only Mother Paul, the superior, had the perk of reading the *Irish Press*. Mickey Gardiner had his hand up: 'Sister Clare! Sister! Hitler came over in an aeroplane to bomb London and wasn't a wing blown off the aeroplane and he had to fly back to Germany on one wing.'

'Goodness gracious,' commented the wide-eyed, elderly nun.

At this stage rumours started circulating about some big military happening – some sort of D-Day – that was going to take place. It was all hush-hush, yet the rumour went round anyway. When various branches of the LDF had a marching competition in Ballybeg, you suspected something was in the offing. Ballybeg, of course, won that competition 'hands down'. The day was carried by the immaculate marching, smart halting and impressive about-turns of Budgie Corcoran and Mick Power.

Next came an impressive show of force with the St Patrick's Day parade, as the serried ranks of LDF, LSF and Red Cross volunteers marched by the reviewing stand, led by commanding officer Paddy Teehan. The bayonets on the rifles glittered in the spring sunshine. All of them had corks stuck on the points to avoid anyone being poked in the eye by accident. As the magnificent force marched down Green Street, Joe Dunne remarked that Hitler would think twice before invading Ballybeg!

The lie was given to this soon after when someone spotted a German submarine in the King's River. Even if it were one of those one-man submarines, this was somewhat odd, because in parts of the river there was scarcely enough water 'to bathe a star', as the poet said. Nevertheless this inspired a great scare and much patrolling of the waterway.

And then 'D-Day' arrived. Extensive manoeuvres were planned for a certain Sunday. They would involve all the volunteer forces around the Kilkenny area. The Ballybeg contingent was assigned the unenviable task of capturing Kilkenny Castle. They would leave the town in the small hours of the morning, march to Ballymack Cross, where they would be met by a truck of the regular army which would supply them with guns. They arrived on time. But no army truck met them with guns at Ballymack. They waited and

DAD'S ARMY

waited, growing more frustrated by the minute. Eventually they secured sticks from the hedgerows to simulate guns and, thus armed, set out for the conquest of Kilkenny Castle. The army lorry, having mistaken the rendezvous, had stopped at a crossing further on at Ballybur. Since no volunteers arrived, they went back to Kilkenny on back roads to avoid 'enemy' troops.

The Ballybeg contingent advanced on Kilkenny and with their sticks stormed the castle. A fierce fight ensued, but the force from Ballybeg won the day. Just as the GPO in Dublin bears the bullet marks of the 1916 Rising, so does Kilkenny Castle have splinters of wood embedded in it from that momentous day. Jim Brien scaled a wall and got himself into the castle garden, where he hid behind a shrub. Eventually three top-brass military men strolled up the garden, consulting maps and talking strategy. Imagine their amazement when Jim jumped out from behind a bush and held them up with a stick. 'Hands up! Surrender!'

When they demurred, he declared, 'Come on now, fair is fair, I had you covered all the way up the garden and could have shot you at any time.' The general looked wryly at the stick and turned to his two officers. 'Will somebody get this eejit out of here?' he demanded.

Then, at last, came the end of the war and of the 'Emergency' too. People forgot warlike activities and began to dream of snow-white bread and loads of tea, sugar and butter. Mickey Croke's shop was the first to display oranges again. They caused great excitement, particularly among the children. As for myself, I asked, 'If oranges come, can bananas be far behind?'

With hostilities over, the government turned its attention to a general election about that time. The politicians addressed the people of Ballybeg from the top of the steps that led up to the Town Hall. With some other children, I was on those steps looking out at the throng gathered below. Tom Walsh was speaking and lauding the efforts of the government to feed the Irish population during the war. 'We gave you bread!' he cried – he was quite an orator. 'But we have no butter!' shouted Mick Joyce from the middle of the crowd. This was greeted with peals of laughter. Slightly deflated, Tom assured him, 'We'll give you butter too.' A resilient people, the people of Ballybeg.

So Passes Worldly Glory

A solid citizen, Tom eked a sparse living from the difficult tract of land he called his farm. Unrelenting toil and the passing years taught him wisdom. On one point he was adamant. There are seven days in the week and never a valid reason for working on the Lord's Day. Even in the wettest of harvest times, when just about everyone worked to get the crops in, he never veered from his principle and, as luck would have it, was always able to demonstrate that it was true.

When he was quite old yet still working on his land, but with the occasional help of a nephew now, I met him. It was in an eating house on a fair day; both of us were enjoying a hearty meal of bacon and cabbage. Though getting on, his abundant hair was still remaining stubbornly black, yet flecked here and there with the odd silver strand. Only the craggy face hinted at the long years he had been on the road.

Having washed down his meal with a satisfying pint of Guinness, he grew pensive. We chatted about farming and about the current problem of saving the crops owing to bad weather. People were availing of every chance they got, some even on Sundays. I opined that it was understandable in the circumstances. Tom did not disagree with me – he was not a man to force his beliefs upon you. Instead, intermittently puffing on his pipe, he told me a story.

'As a young man I gave a spell working for a farmer in County Offaly. In that neighbourhood, there was a Big House with an extensive farm, a domain really. And you know something, the people in that house didn't have a thought for anything except makin money. They worked very hard; I'll hand them that. But every day was the same to them, whether it was Sunday or Monday, made no difference. I was down there again not so long ago of a dark windy day and, God bless the mark, that house is now a ruin. Crows were flyin in and out the windows. Isn't life a quare ould thing.

So passes worldly glory.

Ghosts I

I cannot now remember what season it was when my mother and aunties, Nan and Rita, sat round a blazing fire and scared the daylights out of one another with their ghost stories. It certainly wasn't summer, because the night was dark, overcast and chilly outside. I myself, a lad of about ten at the time, was equally scared at these yarns that went on compulsively, each one eliciting another, if possible more terrifying.

'There was this tall man that used to be seen at night along the road up near Kilbride cemetery,' began Nan. 'All dressed up he was with top hat, dickybow, a carnation in his lapel and his polished shoes shinin in the light of the moon. He usually appeared on moonlit nights.'

'Why did he haunt that road?' Rita wondered.

'They say,' Nan continued, 'that in years gone by a young couple was gettin married up that way. The bridegroom was waitin for the bride who was being driven to the church in a side-car, but didn't the horse bolt and wasn't she thrown from the car and died of a broken neck, God between us and all harm.'

The drastic revelation was met with a stunned silence.

'Instead of a marriage there was a sad funeral as she was laid to rest in her wedding dress in Kilbride cemetery. They say the husband-to-be never did an hour's good after that and died later of a broken heart. And now he forever walks the road, waiting for his beautiful bride. He's been seen by many down the years.'

As though to confirm this, Rita said, 'They say that Biddy Doyle saw an elegantly dressed man one moonlit night while walking past the graveyard. Remember Biddy? She was still alive when we were childer, a sort of woman-of-the-roads. An awful curious woman, they say she was. Well, as she passed near Kilbride cemetery, she spotted the man reading a newspaper by the light of the moon. Nothing would do her but to go up to him and say: "Haven't ye the great eyesight to be able to read by the light of the moon." At this the man vanished. Biddy wasn't in the better of it for months. It was probably that poor spirit who lost his bride.'

In the moments of silence that followed, there was a gentle moan of wind and the front door rattled slightly.

'Talk about graveyards, but many people say they'd rather be locked in a graveyard at night than in a church. Strange to say that's supposed to be the worst place of all to be caught in,' said Nan.

'I heard of a man who was prayin in a church one night,' Nan went on, 'and, when he decided to go out, he found he was locked in. He was really frightened, and not without reason. During the night, the lights were suddenly switched on in the sanctuary and a priest came out from the sacristy fully vested for Mass. He turned round on the altar and asked if there was anyone present who could serve his Mass. Although he was trembling all over, the man went up and served the Mass. When the church was opened the following morning, his fine head of black hair had gone snow white, God bless the mark. You see the priest had died without sayin a Mass he had been paid to say and was comin back to say it. That was in ould God's time when a priest couldn't say a Mass without a server.'

'And sure wasn't there a woman in our own town of Ballybeg long ago that also got locked in the church,' noted Rita.

'Yes, I remember hearin about that,' said Nan. 'For some reason or other, she went into the confession box to pray and fell asleep there and the sacristan, not thinking there was anyone in the building, locked her in. When she awoke in the night, whatever she saw, she must have panicked, because she jumped out through one of the windows. What she didn't seem to know was that there was a big drop by the side of the church. Somehow, although she was badly injured, she managed to struggle home and was heard moanin on the doorstep – where she died.'

'Bab, do you believe in ghosts?' asked Rita of my mother who had listened to all the foregoing without saying a word.

'I think it's all pishogues,' she said, but not convincingly because she went on to add to the pishogues. 'Remember our neighbour, poor Joe Fitzgerald, when we were only childer?'

'Yes.'

'Well, one long summer evening as darkness was at last beginning to fall, he was standing outside his door listening intently to something. Then he asked me, "Can you hear her?"'

"Who, Joe?"

"The banshee, cryin down in the Blind Boreen."

"I can't hear a thing, Joe."

"But her wailin is as clear as clear can be," he added with a look of fear in his eyes.

'Since I could hear nothing, I think he understood the call was for him. He died not long after, leavin a wife and young family.'

Duly awe-stricken, everyone seemed to huddle closer together and move nearer to the fire. In retrospect I realise that this was the implicit purpose of the whole event – family solidarity and community. In the era before television, the hearth was the core of cohesion; and the immediacy of it all made the experience far more satisfying than television. Sometimes the experience was filled with laughter, other times people loved being scared out of their wits.

'We've all had our say now, except Jim,' said Nan. 'Have you got anything to tell us?'

'I was sleepin upstairs at Nanny's and I woke up during the night. I turned over to go back to sleep, but I couldn't and I began to be very afraid and I didn't know why. I was awake for a long time and I was sweatin because I was afraid. Then I heard heavy steps begin at the far end of the room and come very quickly across to me bed, gettin louder all the time. They stopped at the side of me bed. Me heart was poundin, so it was. I peeped up in the darkness. I thought I could see someone standin over me. I wasn't sure. I couldn't sleep any more that night and I was longin for daylight ...'

There was silence when I finished and the group was looking at me in surprise. This was a story about their own home. Rita whispered to the others and I caught the phrase 'not the only one'.

'Is this true, Jim?' asked my mother.

'Yes, Mammy.'

'Then why didn't you tell me about it before.'

'I was afraid the man would come an' kill me if I told anyone.'

'So it was a man?'

'I suppose so. The boots were heavy.'

'You should have told me about it. If anything like that ever happens again you must let me know.'

'OK, Mammy.'

They obviously found my story disturbing – it hit close to home. Maybe that was why, needing some solace, they talked of soon putting on the kettle to make the tea. As preparations were made for the tea, there were some more tales of ghosts, goblins, faery funerals, mysterious knocking on doors...

The evening seemed to be coming to a satisfactory close with the breaking of soda bread and the consumption of cheering tea. That was until my Auntie Rita spoke. 'Now,' she announced, 'after all them ghost stories, I'm afraid to go home by meself' – she lived in Ballybeg, about a mile away.

'Don't worry,' my mother said, 'Jim will go with you.'

Jim will go with you. Has my mother gone mad, I wondered. It wasn't accompanying Auntie Rita to the edge of the town that intimidated me; what petrified me was the prospect of returning home along that sepulchral road.

'Would you mind, Jim?' enquired Rita. 'You won't be afraid, will you?'

Afraid. Don't be ridiculous. I'm the man around here (my father was working in England at the time). And, although my heart had sunk to my boots, I replied valiantly, 'Not at all.'

On the way to Ballybeg, Rita chatted amiably with me and as soon as the street lamps appeared on the edge of the town, she said, 'I'll be all right from here. You can go home now, boy. And thanks.'

Don't even mention it, Aunt Rita, I thought discreetly to myself. Of course she would be all right, but what about me!

I began the daunting journey home with the relish of a mutinous sailor walking the plank. Very soon I was in dark places, passing a lonely farmhouse, on an eminence surrounded by age-old trees, an eerie place that an imaginative brother of mine had named Wuthering Heights. As I went down the incline from this place, I was accompanied by a sobbing in the trees that seemed

GHOSTS I

like pursuing spirits. Did I hear footsteps? I looked behind and with narrowed eyes tried to penetrate the almost totally black night. I could see nothing, but felt it was on such a night that spirits walked abroad and planets struck.

As I turned into the boreen that led to my home, I began to breathe more easily, but it was then that I met my greatest challenge. I saw a candle gliding hauntingly towards me in the night. Nearer and nearer it came without an accompanying sound. Unable to move, I was beginning to falter at the knees. Then a voice said, 'Goodnight boy!' It was Bridie Rochford padding the road in her soft shoes – to ease her acute arthritis – on the way to town on some late night errand. 'Oh Bridie, if you hadn't spoken I'd have dropped dead with the fright.' In response she gave her hearty cackle of a laugh. To light her way she was – oddly – carrying a candle in a jam jar.

Gratefully, I staggered in the door of our house.

All of that happened well-nigh seventy years ago. A lifetime really. Ghosts don't seem to have the same currency anymore. Do I believe in ghosts? Well, yes and no. I believe in ghosts as figments of our imaginations, not as something objectively out there. If I am fixated with someone that has passed away, I may well see that person. However, they are not there. This is why the phantoms never communicate. There are, of course, myriad paranormal happenings that are difficult to explain. I feel that there are many conundrums that will be resolved as knowledge grows. However, we are never likely to discover all the answers, because beyond our material world there is a spiritual realm that is largely a foreign 'land'. Hamlet somehow sums it up for me when he says to Horatio:

> There are more things in heaven and earth, Horatio,
> Than are dreamt of in your philosophy.

As for the characters in my story (my mother, Nan, Rita, Bridie Rochford, Biddy Doyle, Joe Fitzgerald) they are all long gone. For them, all the mysteries about ghosts have been resolved – for they are now ghosts themselves.

Ghosts II

It was a small hotel with a pub on the ground floor. Owing to a series of strange occurrences, with time it garnered the reputation of being haunted. For one thing, there was a room which, if left open, gave rise to all sorts of weird phenomena. Hence a succession of proprietors kept it firmly locked. An elderly man of medium height with foam-white hair and beard, clothed in black clothes and bowler hat, appeared about the place on various occasions. I could recall seeing that man once – while he was still alive.

I never dreamed that this situation would impact upon my own life. But it did. As a newly ordained priest, I was visiting the then owner of the hotel who was a school friend of mine. In the course of our conversation, he brought up the subject of the haunting. He mentioned the mysterious room, the spectre of the elderly man and spoke of curious levitations. While in bed at night, he would suddenly wake up and find his bed raised almost to the level of the ceiling. He was obviously finding it all most distressing. I asked him the obvious question as to why he purchased the hotel, considering its dubious reputation. As many down-to-earth people would, he dismissed the tales as pishogues; besides the strategically placed hotel – it was on the main street – and the fact that it also featured a pub seemed to make it a good business proposition. Indeed, for some patrons, the ghostly tales were an added attraction – until they experienced the eerie reality.

The upshot of our conversation was that he asked me to bless the place. I did so without hesitation and it was this that probably proved my undoing, for I seem to have unhinged some spirit in the process.

That very night, I was sitting at the fire chatting with members of my family when, suddenly, something threw itself at the front door with such force that it almost took it off the hinges. We all fell silent and looked at each other – appalled.

'What in God's name was that?' whispered my mother.

We sat there for some moments in stunned silence. Then with pounding heart, I went to investigate. I gingerly opened the door. No one there. Nobody round about. It was a moonlit summer's night. Not a feather stirring. What caused the rumpus at the door? I didn't know then, and I still don't know to this day, yet I had an uncanny feeling that it was somehow linked to my visit to the hotel. The clamour was actually repeated during that same night and was heard by a brother of mine who was returning late from a holiday.

In due course, I went to take up my first appointment as a priest on the island of Malta. I had quite forgotten about the whole strange affair. My bedroom in Malta was part of a large building on the premises of a school, which was built as the nineteenth century gave way to the twentieth. The furnishings reflected the era. My bed was a four-poster, Victorian contraption in which I felt quite lost, but whatever it was that crashed into our door in Ireland succeeded in finding me. I wasn't long in my new home when I was rudely awakened one night by something violently shaking my four-poster. As back in Ireland, I was quite frightened by the event. And it wasn't simply a once-off visitation – it happened again and again. On one occasion, the 'visitor' applied such force that the bed was nearly dragged into the centre of the room. It seemed the presence had pursued me from Ireland.

As the eerie experience was continuously repeated, a strange thing began to happen. My fear of the poltergeist, or whatever it was, disappeared. I would feel my bed rocking and say, 'Oh, not again!' turn over and go back to sleep. I even began to feel on friendly, even playful, terms with the ghost.

Then, it suddenly occurred to me that maybe this spirit was looking for my prayers. How stupid of me not to have thought of this before. The poor soul must have been utterly frustrated with me. I started to pray and, after some time, the nocturnal visits stopped as abruptly as they had begun. I sometimes wonder if my ghostly friend has now forgotten me and that I would appreciate a little farewell shake of a night.

Ghosts III

Two great friends of mine with connections to Ballybeg took their three children, a boy and two girls, for an outing in the Dublin mountains. In the course of it they visited the ruin of the eerie Hell Fire Club. These premises operated in the 1800s and were a place of ill repute. There were rumours of all sorts of dark goings on: wild gambling, drunkenness, womanising ... And there were even reports of Old Nick himself making an appearance on one occasion, presumably because he found this den a congenial theatre of operations. It was no great surprise for upright folk, therefore, when it was eventually destroyed by fire. They merely looked around to see if there was any brimstone involved as well.

After labouring up the steep slope, the parents entered the ruin with a sense of foreboding. After all, they had heard the rumours about the place. To the children, it was just one more historic building to visit; they were told that in the past it was some sort of clubhouse.

As they moved round the various rooms of the building, three-year-old Aoife, the youngest member of the family abruptly announced, 'I died here.' The parents did a double take, yet maintained their composure. Then the father casually asked, 'Here in this room, Aoife?'

'No. Upstairs. There was a fire.'

The astounded parents stopped their mouths from falling open and, moving on, said no more.

A little later, they came into a sizeable room. Said the mother, 'I'd say this was the place where people came to relax, a sitting room.'

'No,' piped up Aoife. 'This was where they played the cards.'

This was too much! Where was this information coming from? The child had no previous knowledge of these matters.

But that was it. From that day to this, Aoife has never again returned to the subject. Indeed she seems quite oblivious of it.

It was passing strange to say the least.

The Miracle

Following closing time at Martin's pub in Ballybeg, Mick Carroll was, as usual, making his way home with his little donkey and cart. Truth to tell, he had overdone the drinking a tad and was feeling quite drowsy and kept nodding off to sleep. There was no great danger really, because the donkey, who bore the uninspired name of Neddy, had long memorised his way home. Also it was during World War II and cars were so scarce that, were one to lie on the road with the intention of committing suicide, they would die first of starvation.

When Neddy arrived at Mick's wayside cottage, he came to a halt. He waited, snorted and gave his bridle a tingling shake, but the only reaction from Mick was a deep snore, so the animal took up his customary resigned stance at the gate.

After a while, a group of young blades came by on bicycles on their way home from Bill Egan's cinema. They weren't making too much noise for fear of the garda, because they had no lamps on their bikes. On coming upon Mick sleeping in his cart, they stopped.

'What will we do?' asked one.

'If it was a good night,' replied another, 'you could just cover him with a sack and leave him there in the arms of Murphy until he wakes up. But I don't like the black look of that sky. Not even a lone star to be seen. I think there could be a downpour.'

'It's in the arms of Morpheus', interjected a third with a smattering of classical knowledge.

'Whatever.'

Having discussed Mick's plight, they decided to get him indoors, but found a creative way to do so. The door of the cottage was of course open. In those days people only locked their doors last thing at night; to do otherwise would be utterly inhospitable. They would probably leave them open all night if they weren't afraid that the pooka might slip in and get up to mischief. Having taken a look at the door of the cottage and found it ample enough, this group of 'tricksters' untackled the donkey, dismantled the tiny cart, transferred everything – donkey included – into the kitchen and reassembled the lot there. The profoundly sleeping Mick they placed gently in the cradle of his cart. Closing the door, they then left, gleefully anticipating his utter bewilderment on awakening in the morning.

Long after daylight had broken, Mick slowly surfaced from a slough of leaden slumber. As his situation dawned on him, he shot upwards following a few failed attempts. 'Mother of God, how did I get here? he queried in amazement. He scrutinised the cart and now drooping donkey for clues. There were none – he was flummoxed. Easing himself ponderously out of the cart, he went to the kitchen window and peered out into the gloom. There had been an apocalyptic deluge in the night. All the signs were there: beleaguered trees, dripping hedgerows, massive pools of water ... He looked back at the slack-eared donkey, standing patiently. No it couldn't have been the donkey, Mick concluded, he didn't have the necessary skills. 'Twas a miracle,' he at last concluded, 'the Blessed Virgin got me inside. If she hadn't I'd have caught double perryapneumonia in that awful rain.' The chorus-sounding diagnosis of the malady that could have befallen him and the high-pitched emphasis he gave the condition left no doubt as to its menace.

The miracle, however, was even more complicated than Mick imagined. Not only did the Blessed Virgin get him inside, but she organised it so that a posse of pranksters would arrive precisely in his hour of dire need. That was neat. Indeed the only flaw in the situation was that the donkey had befouled the floor, which explained his drooping guilty look. But life is never perfect.

Nostalgia

Tom Buggy and Mary Kate Brennan got married in 1923 and after a celebration that lasted most of the night left Ballybeg for Queenstown (now Cobh) to board the ship for New York. Parents, relations and friends set up a wild keening, which implied that never again did they expect to see them on this side of the grave. It truly was an American wake, though the era of American wakes was coming to an end. They were a handsome couple and it was many a maiden that envied Mary Kate her 'lonely' exile with Tom.

They settled in the Bronx. In those days it was a tranquil place inhabited mostly by Irish. You could safely walk the streets after dark or even sleep through a warm summer's night on a park bench. But all their lives Tom and Mary Kate would look fondly back on the hard yet happy days of their youth in Ballybeg. And, as a lifetime tiptoed by, memories of the happiness glowed ever more brightly, fanned by the idealising nostalgia of so many exiles for 'the ould sod', while the memories of hardships seemed to fade away. So after forty-five years, Tom and Mary Kate decided to retire back to Ballybeg.

They said goodbye to the sweat-banded joggers, graffiti-covered trains thundering across iron bridges, fearsome subways, impassive faces, intermittent neon lights – the pastiche that made the violent drug-tormented New York of the 1970s a far cry from the neighbourly place they had come to in the 1920s.

The first thing was to secure a home. This they did without much trouble. It was a comfortable little bungalow on the outskirts – insofar as one could talk of outskirts in a place so small – of Ballybeg.

They then set about trying to meet the friends of their youth in earnest. Not surprisingly, they found their numbers sadly depleted and those who remained had been so ravaged by time that they were obliged to introduce themselves with a voice that sometimes quavered. 'You don't remember me? Many's the time I danced a lancer with ye at Murphy's Cross long ago until Canon Lowry arrived on his white horse to scatter us all ... Bridie Cotter ... I was Bridie Kelly in those days.'

'Ah Bridie, y'old sonofabitch, of course I remember you. How could I forget?'

Being called a sonofabitch left poor Bridie somewhat 'discommoded'. She was ignorant of terms of endearment in the Bronx. Tom was baffled by the subsequent chilling of the atmosphere. 'Did ye hear what the Yank called Bridie Cotter?' The voice went across town like perplexity across a face.

There was one person with whom Tom struck up a great relationship – Paddy Moran who owned a tiny sweet-shop. But then didn't Tom know his father and grandfather, God rest them, both decent men. The two would chat by the hour and Tom invariably invited Paddy to the nearest pub for a pint. Paddy always refused saying that he couldn't possibly because he was chained to 'the business' like Kunta Kinte. Paddy had found out all about Kunta Kinte after a flame-headed travelling woman to whom he had curtly refused largess upbraided him with, 'Go on y'old Kunta Kinte!'

One day Tom returned from a visit to the graveyard beyond the town. He was sad. 'Now I know why I meet so few of the old friends, Paddy. They're all pushin up daisies. The town I knew is transferred to Kilbride.'

Had he forgotten that life over the last forty-five years had been harsher in Ireland than in the States? Paddy wondered.

Ever since returning, there was a little spot below The Mill that Tom and Mary Kate were longing to see. There they had become childhood sweethearts. Down the years and even above the incessant roar of New York, they had often heard the mill-wheel trundling in their souls and pictured the churning foam rapidly change into a lively trout stream. They saw Vaughan's meadow slope gently down to the water's edge and the stepping stones that coaxed one across to the enchantment of Butler's Grove.

Yet, before going, they waited until Maytime, when the hawthorns would be in bloom and the meadow a galaxy of buttercups and daisies. What they found was another shattered dream: the mill-wheel a rusted skeleton, the waters stygian and faintly

NOSTALGIA

smelling of sewage, the meadow and Butler's Grove annihilated. The horns of elfland utterly silent.

With stooped shoulders they walked silently home, hand in hand. Somehow they seemed suddenly older.

Since the companions of his youth were so few, more and more Tom resorted to chatting with Paddy Moran. He reminisced endlessly about Ballybeg at the beginning of the century and about his lifetime in New York. About how the Irish were underpaid and exploited on the tramcars – not even given a break on Sunday morning for Mass. Mike Quill, that great Kerryman, got the union going and put a stop to all that. In 1929, when there was the Great Wall Street Crash, he saw one of the very men who had exploited the Irish standing in a soup queue, God help him. 'Arrah Paddy, I could write a book.'

'Now ye said it. That's the very thing ye must do. It'd be most interesting.' Tom went home elated with the thought of this new project.

The following day he sat down at the sitting-room table with a pen and a sheet of paper. 'In nineteen-twenty-three,' he began, 'I, Tom Buggy and my wife, Mary Kate, of Ballybeg in the county of Kilkenny left our beloved parish to cross what John F. Kennedy referred to, during his visit to Ireland in nineteen-sixty-three, as that bowl of tears called the Atlantic.'

He read the words aloud and liked them - especially the bit about the bowl of tears. Sucking his pen, he began to think. Emotions, images and experiences teemed within him. He set about trying to put shape on these in his mind, but eventually felt somewhat overwhelmed and wearied by the task, so he pushed the sheet of paper into a drawer and called on Mary Kate for a cup of coffee, after which he sauntered down to Paddy for 'a chinwag'.

'How's the book goin, Tom?'

'I've made a start.'

'Good man. Keep at it.'

On leaving Paddy's, Tom ran into the extrovert and genial curate, Father Walsh. 'Are you well, Tom?'

'Fair, father.'

'Meet any more of the old friends?'

'Very few. Though, come to think of it, I really meet them all the time in the faces of the young people who pass me by on the street. But youth today don't seem inclined to want to talk to the old people the way we loved to in my day.'

Father Walsh laughed and, putting a magnanimous hand on Tom's shoulder, rocked him gently. 'Tom, you never stand in the same river twice.'

As for Mary Kate, she did move around a little after returning. Finding old acquaintances so scarce, however, she reverted to her custom of the Bronx and stayed mostly indoors. Besides, she discovered that in the end their present preoccupations and the experiences of a lifetime distanced her irrevocably from childhood friends. There's only so much you can say about old times. Indeed she was now dreaming of those friends she had left behind in New York. Of the coffee mornings and bridge parties at the Sacred Heart.

With a flash of womanly intuition she said to Tom one day, 'We left behind in the Bronx what we came looking for here. Let's cut our losses and go back and find it again.' Tom wasn't so sure it was that easy. The words of the genial Father Walsh kept ringing in his ears, 'You never stand in the same river twice.' You could freeze a film but not life.

Despite his misgivings he and Mary Kate sold their bungalow and returned to the Bronx. No slow boat this time – a jumbo jet from Shannon. Within three months, Tom was dead.

A mortuary card announcing the death reached Paddy Moran in due course. Also enclosed was a pound note. 'While going through Tom's things,' explained Mary Kate, 'I found this Irish punt in his pocket and I thought you might like to have it.'

Paddy looked ruefully at the note. 'What am I expected to do with this?' he asked. On his counter there was a box marked 'Salesian Missions', so with difficulty he stuffed it in there. 'I wish that priest would come around sometime and empty this yoke. It's been full to the gills for months.'

The bungalow was bought by a Mr Cahill, a retired bank manager and a widower. One day while eventually settling in, he opened the drawer of the sitting-room table and found a sheet of paper with something written on it. 'In nineteen-twenty-three,' he read, 'I, Tom Buggy and my wife, Mary Kate, of Ballybeg in the county of Kilkenny left our beloved parish to cross what John F. Kennedy referred to, during his visit to Ireland in nineteen-sixty-three, as that bowl of tears called the Atlantic.'

'Umph,' said Cahill, 'some bowl.' and threw it into the fire. The paper burned and writhed yet struggled to survive. The words were still discernible on the charred sheet. Then Cahill poked the fire and those words succumbed at last, crumbled to ashes, and were lost forever.

Little Unremembered Acts

That best portion of a good man's life,
His little, nameless, unremembered acts
Of kindness and of love.
William Wordsworth

The first day I went to school, I never got there. Not by a long shot. There I was with my 'shining morning face' and brown canvas bag slung across my shoulder. I got to the door of our home in Mill Street, Ballybeg, urged on by my mother and grandparents, but then had second thoughts. 'I'll go tomorrow I said.' I can't remember anyone seriously demurring. It was Wordsworth who also said, 'The child is father to the man,' and what I did that morning was quite typical of my life. I was never one to rush into things.

Next day, though full of pent-up tears, I went without a murmur.

I had two teachers that day: Sister Virgilius and Sister Oliver. In later life I became good friends with both. They were to devote long years of service as nurses in St Luke's Hospital, Kilkenny. While waiting to begin their training as nurses, they were given the infants' class to look after at the convent school, Ballybeg.

My first day at school was bitterly cold. I felt miserable and on the verge of weeping. Aware of this, Sister Virgilius sat me by the fire and handed me a bar of chocolate; one of those neat little Cadbury bars so popular in the thirties. While I was being singled out for this special treatment, Sister Oliver had the other children, who must have looked at me with envy, sing 'Ta Nead ag Maire'.

While I sat cosily by the fire, someone could be heard screaming in the distance. I didn't have to be told who it was. It was my neighbour, Jimmy Walsh, who started school a few weeks before me and never took to it. Every day his mother, Biddy, had to drag him kicking and screaming there. The main reason why I managed to restrain my own tears was that I didn't want to be branded 'a crybaby like Jimmy Walsh'. But maybe Jimmy was wiser to let it all hang out, as the Americans say.

I vaguely remember Jimmy being sat at the fire with me, which would have been appropriate, because we became good friends in the years that followed. There were in fact two Jimmy Walshes in our class: James Walsh 1 and James Walsh 2. James Walsh 2 was the person sitting by the fire with me; James Walsh 1, also a friend, was destined to become a renowned boxer and also a useful hurler.

That morning is, of course, etched forever on my memory, especially the kindness of Sisters Virgilius and Oliver. Seventy years later Sister Virgilius passed away in her nineties and on the way back to Dublin from her funeral the following little poem came to me, so I pulled off the road and wrote it down.

Little nameless, unremembered acts ...
The day was really bitter
when first I went to school
and I a lonely little boy
all frozen and forlorn –
then sister sat me by the fire
and handed me a chocolate bar.
Though seventy years have seeped away
like waves on sandy shore,
that fire still warms my heart,
that chocolate cheers my soul.

The Road Less Travelled

He simply couldn't grasp it. But the stark phrases would not go away: 'Killed on Thursday 5th inst. [a neat local paper touch, he thought] ... Ford Cortina in collision with an articulated lorry deeply regretted by her loving husband and children ...'

Back wandered his mind to a golden summer almost thirty years before. Sunny day followed sunny day with the inexorability of waves rolling in on a strand. That year he was helping an old farmer called Stephen and there were acres of hay to be saved, but it was dry and honey-yellow and light as gossamer on the glinting steel of the pitchfork.

At about noon each day Stephen's doughty wife, Molly, would come with refreshments. First of all there was a jug of water with oatmeal at the bottom to keep it cool; then there was steaming tea and hearty sandwiches. After hours of arduous work these refreshments were welcome indeed. Even now, all these years later, his mouth watered at the very thought of them.

As each day's haymaking ended, the cows had to be hand-milked and the liquid sang in the zinc buckets as it was jettisoned from overladen teats. Then followed a well-earned supper.

That was the unbroken pattern of each day. Apart, that is, from the day Mary appeared. She came at noon carrying the refreshments instead of Molly. Suddenly he looked up and saw a lissome girl of sixteen with golden hair and warm blue eyes.

'Ah Mary,' said Stephen with evident pleasure, 'tis yerself. Yer welcome. What good wind blew you this way? This is Mary, me niece. And this young lad here is called Liam.'

'Nice to meet you,' he said shyly.

'You too,' she replied. 'Mammy sent me to Auntie Molly with some patterns,' she answered Stephen's original question.

Ah so that was it. He was wondering how she could be a niece to one so old as Stephen. But Molly was twenty years younger than her husband and probably sister to the girl's mother.

THE ROAD LESS TRAVELLED

'How're the holidays goin, girl? I hope they're not workin you too hard in the shop. Yer father is an awful man for the money an with you servin an' turnin all the young fellas heads up there in Ballingarry there'll be terrible consumption of icecream an lemonade.'

Laughing, she glanced at the boy. He blushed. Then felt a fool. He was nearly eighteen, damn it.

'Won't ye have a cup of tay yourself, Mary? You sir, pour the young lady a cup of tay.'

'No thank you, uncle. I've had some.'

'Ah come on, just a cup in yer hand.' She accepted. The old man who could be quiet and saturnine was blossoming in the presence of this beautiful girl.

'Mary, the nuns are teachin ye powerful manners altogether. You're not makin a sound drinkin that tay. An' you talk real swanky too. Look at the young lad there, frozen in your presence.'

It was true. How 'the young lad' wished he too had been trained by the nuns, instead of being an uncouth brothers' boy.

'Arrah go on outa that, uncle,' she broke into the vernacular.

'Somehow I don't think yer goin to spend your life milkin cows an' feedin chickens like your poor Aunt Molly.'

'What's wrong with milking cows and feeding chickens?'

'Farmin is pure hardship, girl. Don't have anythin to do with fellas that make hay.'

She stole an amused glance at the boy. 'Why didn't you give that advice to Aunt Molly, uncle?'

'It would have done no good. She was blinded by love.'

Again she laughed and gathered the utensils. When she left, the edge of brightness seemed to go off the summer's day.

Eventually the long weeks of toil came to an end and were transformed into a neatly trimmed rick of gold in the barn.

The lad and Stephen sat down to a celebratory supper served by the redoubtable Molly, 'Put that inside yer shirts and it won't matter where the night'll fall on ye,' she said.

After supper the boy excused himself and went outside. The sun had gone down and the long twilight had begun. A slight mist was creeping along the meadows. Far up in the crystalline sky the swallows darted and drifted about. The flies are high, he thought. More good weather.

He lowered his eyes from the sky. The moths were beginning to flit about the harebells in the hedgerow. The scent of fresh hay attracted him to the barn to review the result of all the arduous work. How he gazed at it with deep satisfaction.

Somebody tapped him gently on the shoulder. It was Mary.

'You gave me a start.'

'Sorry.' And she tossed her head and gave that musical laugh.

'Haven't seen you for a long time.'

'It's only a week since I was down.'

He was blushing again.

'Mammy sent me with a note to Auntie Molly and Uncle Stephen. It says that the Carrolls have dropped out of Father McCarthy's pilgrimage to Lourdes and now with the hay saved maybe they can come. And who knows but Uncle Stephen's lumbago may be cured. But Mammy says the miraculous water is so cold it'll probably stop his heart while curing his lumbago.'

'Well, Lourdes is probably a better idea than that quack Pat Sweeney. He walked all over his back a month ago saying Hail Marys en route. Funny, immediately after the exercise Stephen said he felt better. But you should have heard him the day after in the hayfield:

"That blasted Sweeney," he ranted, "him an' his big feet an' Hail Marys. Me back is worse than ever." ' He was surprised to find himself beginning to talk so freely to her.

'Father McCarthy is offering them a reduced rate.'

'That should help,' he said.

She giggled. 'You're quick.'

'No, just experienced. If I were smart I'd not be here.'

'They are stingy aren't they?'

'Not with buttermilk, bacon an' eggs, griddle cake, jam ... with money, yes. I'd swear that when old Steve unties his purse strings, moths fly out.'

'By the way, Mammy and Daddy are going to Lourdes, but I'm not ... If aunt and uncle go, will you be looking after the place here?'

'No – sadly – I finish this week.'

There was a long silence. Once again he became conscious of the distant twittering of the swallows. Down in the fields the nervous dexter lowed querulously as the evening continued to fade imperceptibly.

'It's true then?' she asked.

'What?'

'That you're going away to study, over in England.'

'Yes.'

'You've thought hard about it?'

'I have.'

'Must you go then?'

'I must.'

'So it's like that ... I'm glad and I'm sorry.'

He looked earnestly at her. It was her turn to blush.

He lowered his head. Brown wavy hair dropped over his forehead. He scuffed the dust with his toe. And then, almost without knowing what he was doing, kissed her gently on the cheek.

Somewhat confused, he muttered, 'I'm going down the fields to look at the animals,' and left her. Never did he see the tear that had gathered in her eye.

***

Once more he looked at the newspaper. At the photo of the family gathered by the graveside. The boys with one possible exception took after the father. Not so Mary, the only girl. Even in black and white the likeness was not just unmistakable, it was uncanny. He could picture the sheen of the hair, the deep blue of those affectionate eyes.

The sights and sounds of an interminable summer thirty years ago came crowding back: flimsy hay in neat swards, drowsy days laden with the hum of nectar-seeking bees, warm milk singing in buckets, the swallows, hunkered-down rabbits nibbling in the rosy fields of evening.

There were footsteps.

'Ah, Sifiso.'

'Good night.'

'You should carry your torch. The snakes are moving about with this warm weather. I'd most certainly have stepped on a cobra last night, if I hadn't had mine.'

'Is it?'

'Did you manage to get some petrol for the jeep?'

'Yes, half.'

'OK, then, we'll start for Ezulwini. We'd better get a good night's rest. That road is *rud eile*.'

'*Umfundisi?*'

'That road is something else, rugged.'

'Oh ... Mr Shongwe was here to get a sack of mealies. He'd like a lift back to Ezulwini.'

'That'll be fine provided that he doesn't turn up with the extended family and ten sacks of mealies.'

'Stay well *umfundisi.*'

'Go well, Sifiso, and greet Joyce and the children for me.'

Standing up, he dropped the *Kilkenny People* to the floor and stood vacantly gazing into space. A cockroach ventured gingerly on to the newspaper, stopped, searched about with keen antennae, and shot across its broad expanse. Words of Frost drifted into his mind:

'I shall be telling this with a sigh ... Two roads diverged ... I took the one less travelled by.'

At last, sighing deeply, he resolutely bolted the mission door against the dangers of the night.

A Near Thing

The sparrow, famished after the harsh winter, pecked away at some seedlings on the crest of a grassy bank beneath the eaves of the farmhouse. Blissfully unaware of the cat that stealthily bellied up the slope towards her. The cat by contrast was sleek and shiny, thanks to a plentiful diet of birds, frozen into sluggishness by frost and snow.

Centimetre by centimetre, body disciplined and taut, the feline edged towards the crest. Spotting the danger, the sparrow's mate alighted on the eaves overhead and raised the alarm with a persistent, high-pitched cheep-cheep-cheep ...

But the befuddled bird paid no attention whatsoever. On the contrary she went on pecking away blithely at the feast which, inexplicably, the other sparrows left to her.

First the ears, then the eyes of the cat imperceptibly insinuated themselves above the ridge. The cock-sparrow went frantic. Even risked his life by fluttering momentarily down towards his loved one.

The animal, seeing his predatory intentions frustrated, raised his head slightly to glance at the interloper and shot out a tentative paw, boxer-like. Yet not even then did the hapless bird take warning, so intent was she on her meal. And the cat resumed a tense hunting position. Then came the pounce. The victim screeched in terror and spread her wings. She was actually in flight when transfixed by lethal claws.

Desolate and plaintively cheeping, the cock-sparrow sat for a long time on the eaves of the house. Eventually the cheeping subsided. Slowly he preened his feathers. And then flew away to get on with the rest of his life.

Waiting for Kathleen

'The five of trumps!' shouted a lean man with eager eyes in triumph, decisively slapping his card down on the table.

'No beatin that, Jack,' responded another man. He had a care worn face and a cap pulled down over abundant grey hair. 'It was close though, only one trick. We're one helluva partnership, Jack.'

'You can say that again, Paddy. One more game, lads?'

'I've had enough,' said a burly fellow, 'and if you'd make the drop of tay, I'd have it and be on me way. I think the dexter is goin to calf tonight.'

'I'll be goin too,' said a fair-haired lad. 'I have to say hello to the ould moth, you know.' And he rose to leave.

'Assha wait for a cup of tay, at least,' pleaded Paddy, the host.

'All right, but make it snappy.'

Paddy hung the kettle on the hook over the fire, got down on his knees and blew the turf to a yellow and blue flame. 'Anyone like a bit of soda bread with country butter? Jack there brought a lovely home-baked soda cake.'

'Sure won't we all have a hearty slice,' replied the burly man.

***

With tea over and the others gone, Paddy, the host, and Jack, his lifelong friend and sterling partner in cards, settled down in chairs on either side of the fire and quickly lit their pipes. For some moments they puffed away contentedly. Jack regarded his companion with what seemed an anticipatory smile playing about his eyes.

'Jack, would you credit it–'

'Credit what, Paddy?' interrupted Jack eagerly.

'The man himself sat in that very chair you are sittin on thirty and five long years ago this very month.'

'Who was that, Paddy?'

Paddy puffed philosophically on his pipe, as Jack waited in gleeful expectation.

'For Chrissake, Paddy, who?'

'Now we're both members of the Archconfraternity of the Holy Family, I'd ask you to kindly mind your language.' And he gave a little glance at the Sacred Heart picture with the red oil lamp wavering before it.

'But, Paddy, who on earth sat there? Tell me or I'll bust.'

This prospect seemed to please, Paddy.

He slowly removed the pipe from his mouth and fixed the slavering Jack with a steady gaze. 'None other than the Big Fella himself.'

'De Valera?'

'De Valera,' exclaimed Paddy with a note of disdain. 'He wasn't the Big Fella; he was the Long Fella.'

'Ah, Michael Collins,' declared Jack with satisfaction.

'Who else?' asked Paddy abruptly. 'Our greatest revolutionary … sat right in that spot where you are sittin thirty and five years ago, so he did. Right in the spot where you're sittin.'

'I didn't know that Michael Collins was on the run in Kilkenny.'

'Sure wasn't he on the run everywhere. Isn't that what bein on the run means. When you're on the run you get an awful long way. Take yourself, Jack. If you start runnin now, where'll you be in three days? Answer me that.'

'With me arthritis the way it is, I'd still be here in Ballybeg.'

'Ah, but if you didn't have the old arthritis, if you could run like you did when you played hurlin for Ballybeg, I tell you, Jack, you'd be at the other end of Ireland. But February thirty and five years ago he sat where you are sittin this minute. I remember it was February because the snowdrops were peepin up through the fresh grass out there and the little yellow buds were beginning to form on the daffodils. It was round the feast of Brigid and there was that little somethin in the air. Spring had come early that year. Of course it wasn't generally known that he was around. Just a few of the boys and meself knew … Anyway, "Mick," says I, "I know you're not here for the good of your health. Just tell me what you want and your wishes will be commands for me."

"Paddy," says he, "you divined me thoughts exactly. You're a man who has risked his life many a time and oft for his country, and," says he, "I hesitate to ask any more sacrifices from you, but I don't know where to turn and–'

"General," I interrupted – the moment bein kinda too solemn to say just Mick – "don't say another word. Just give the command."

"This is a highly dangerous mission, captain," says he, promotin me on the spot. You're used to danger, I know, but nevertheless I'm not goin to command you. There's a submarine comin into Tramore with a load of arms for the boys and I want you to get over to Tipperary and ask Dinny Lacey and his men to meet me in Tramore three nights from now at the usual rendezvous, so that we can unload the shipment and continue the fight for Irish freedom."'

'But isn't Tramore a bit shallow for a submarine to come in?' said a mischievous Jack.

Paddy gave him a long indignant look and puffed on his pipe three times, as though to intimate that, if he puffed on his pipe three times, the argument was over. Then he continued, 'As I was sayin, I went and did that little job for Mick and those arms were used to take the Custom House in Dublin and that was the beginnin of the end for the British Empire, so it was.'

'Begob, Paddy, you were really involved with history. I had no idea.'

'Arrah, Jack, you don't know the half of it.' Paddy was growing even more animated. 'Would you believe it, while all on me mother's side were involved in the fight for freedom here at home, all of me father's people answered the call of John Redmond to fight for the freedom of small nations in the August '14 War. Sure didn't I go and give the boys a hand meself at the Battle of the Somme.'

'Tell us about it, Paddy.'

''Twas hell. In the trenches, up to your neck in muck and water, waitin for the order to go over the top and engage Gerry hand to hand. An' the rats…big as greyhounds and I'm not exaggeratin–'

'Perish the thought, Paddy.'

'I remember an almighty rat catchin a poor fella be the name of

Murphy from Cork be the throat and didn't the fella try to drag him away, but sure wasn't he only draggin the throat out of himself, so I knocked him unconscious, bayoneted the rat and I declare to God, Jack, I had to prise his teeth apart to get him away from the young lad's throat. Them were terrible times. It always seemed to be rainin and dark and cold and the land full of barbed wire and jagged, blasted trees like, for all the world, somethin you'd see in a nightmare...And I'll tell you a good one.'

'No better man, Paddy.'

'I was billeted with the Royal Irish Regiment for a while. They used to move me around as the need arose. There were some Kerry fellas – cute divils if ever I met them – who used to play a trick on the Germans. You see a Kerry lad would shout out "*Hans!*" – that's a common German name – and a German would pop his head out of a trench and shout back "*Ya!*" – that's the German for 'What do you want?' – and the Kerryman would pick him off. Of course after a while the Germans cottoned on to this and said these Irish'll find out that they have opened a Panacea's box for themselves, and so they made a plan. They found out that the most common name among the Irish was Paddy, so didn't one of them shout "*Paddy*", and didn't the Kerry fella keep his head down and shout back, "*That you Hans?*" "*Ya*", cried poor Hans, poppin up his head ...'

Jack howled with laughter.

'Ah, Jack, the whole thing was far from bein a laughin matter though. I remember we went over the top one day and I was engagin this German in hand to hand combat and didn't I knock the rifle out of his hands. I was about to bayonet him when I got a fair look at his face. He was little more than a chap and had a look of total panic. I thought of me mother and said to meself that he too was some mother's son and I just couldn't kill him, so I just gave him a kick in th'arse – I mean the backside – and sent him back to his own lines. Afterwards, the captain said that if we all took to kickin Germans in the backsides, instead of killing them, the war would last a helluva long time. Of course there were no great hard feelings between the Germans and the Irish. After all, hadn't we been fightin the British Empire since the time of Brian Boru. One

Christmas didn't all the lads, Irish and German, get out of the trenches and have a hooley together, so they did. There was no hard feelings like. Do you know what I mean? Lord, but they were quare times. Young lads out there dyin when they should have been at home courtin. They missed the women somethin awful. I suppose that was why they sent Gracie Fields out to sing for us.'

'I thought she was around about the time of the Second World War, Paddy?'

Paddy puffed on his pipe three times. "As I was sayin, Gracie Fields came out to sing for us.'

'That must have done somethin to take away the troops' loneliness, but I thought Gracie Fields came a bit later.'

'Jack I'm going to tell you somethin now that you won't fully understand since you still have your Brigid, but going through life without a wife is a hard old station. No one knows better than meself. I never got over ... Kathleen.'

Knowing how true this was, a sad Jack fell silent.

After a while, Paddy resumed. 'Not that I couldn't have married.' Jack knew this to be true also. 'I remember the time I was in Americay, in New York itself, as a matter of fact,' Paddy was off again, 'and didn't I meet this lassie and wasn't she makin it up to me. But I gave her the slip, left New York and went out West. There I had to take wagon trains across the prairies, just like you'd see at the Gaiety in town.'

'I thought all that happened in the last century,' Jack again interrupted his host.

And once more Paddy transfixed him with a censorious look and fell to puffing on his pipe. 'Jack, sometimes you let your imagination run away with you.'

Jack kept a straight face.

'As I was sayin, there was this day when we had to take a wagon train through a deep canon–'

'You mean canyon, Jack.'

'Aye, canon. Well, as evening fell, we stopped at the mouth of the canon, knowin that the hills on either side were bristlin with Injuns: Sioux, Apaches, Pawnees, Cherokees, Gurkees and Zulus.'

Jack refrained from correcting him. Why spoil a good story?

'Well, the leader of the train called me and says he, "Paddy, I want you to take a sizeable possum tonight and try and divart all them Indians, so that I can get the wagon train through the canon in the mornin. The US Calvary contingent will stay with us in case we need protection as we go through."

"Well, sir," says I, "it's a dangerous thing you're asking me to do and no mistake, but there's women and childer in them thar wagons, so I reckon I'll do me doggone best" – wasn't I pickin up the jargon?'

"Paddy O'Hare," he says. "Every night I kneels be me bed and thanks God that you're with this party. Good luck. Whether we live or die is in your hands."

'While it was still dark, not long before daybreak, with much shoutin and hollerin and thunderous gallopin of hooves the possum tore off in the opposite direction from the canon, as if the whole outfit was making a desperate attempt to escape. The wagons were in fact well hidden behind huge rocks. I heard afterwards that the injuns were slow to respond. They were caught unawares as they rested. By the time they regrouped, we were well away. But, eventually, with waving tomahawks and wild whooping they all gave chase. As morning broke, the wagon train, proudly flanked by the US Calvary passed safely through the canon.'

'Great story, Paddy. That surely was some "divarsion". Thank you.'

'Ah don't mention it.'

'And now I must tear meself away, Paddy, or Brigid will be wonderin what has become of me. She'll be filing for divorce!'

'Good night, Jack. Bless yourself with the holy water before you go.'

He left Paddy with his memories, searching deep amid the still glowing embers of the fire. What memories, thought Jack, as he walked home in the faint light of a million stars. The lovely Kathleen, whom he was about to marry, being swept away by consumption. He never got over that. And never had eyes for another woman. Sometimes, he would quietly say, 'I'm waiting for

Kathleen.' They say the loss unhinged his mind a bit. What with the grieving and trying to wring a livelihood from his arid little farm, his life was indeed 'a hard old station'. No wonder he took refuge in the land of the imagination – life in the real world was too harsh. He, Jack, understood him perfectly and, while he got great amusement from the stories, he had the utmost affection and respect for Paddy. You see, he remembered the young man. And he too remembered Kathleen.

Incident by the Somme

Uncle Tom was a gentle giant. Strictly speaking, he wasn't my uncle, but he was married to my aunt Bridie, so he was an adopted uncle. He spoke sparingly and in a soft voice. My siblings and I loved going to his house, where there always seemed to be cuddly puppies and kittens, and in his back garden there grew an abundance of succulent gooseberries and blackcurrants. We were given free rein there.

It was the time of World War II and Tom and Bridie had, for that era, a rare and precious possession – a wireless. I'd often see Tom cycling home from Ballybeg with the dry batteries on the carrier of his bike. Not that Bridie needed a wireless, for, if Tom was a silent man, she was an incessant talker. Maybe that explained his silence. As for Bridie, I think the poor woman kept on talking to keep her mind off the 'ould arthuritis' that afflicted her severely. Now Tom and Bridie didn't keep the wireless to themselves, but were most generous in allowing neighbours in to listen to it. There were, of course, a few more wirelesses in the area, but the populace favoured Rochford's (Tom and Bridie's surname). Tom Dooley declared that it was the only machine you could rely on to tell the truth.

A knot of neighbours would cluster round the apparatus late at night to hear the offerings of William Joyce, alias Lord Haw Haw, on 'Germany Calling'. One night they were disconcerted to hear him say that there would be consequences if the Irish kept on exporting food to England. And he advised the staff at Mullinavat Creamery to keep their butter at home to fatten the Kilkenny hurlers for the All Ireland. The listeners laughed, but it was near the bone. The German knowledge of local culture and topography was disturbing – Mullinavat was just down the road. It was as if the kitchen had just been invaded by men in square helmets.

Speaking of the All Ireland, so many came to listen to the commentaries on the All Ireland Hurling Final – especially if it featured

Kilkenny – that the radio had to be taken out into the backyard to accommodate everyone. Those were magical occasions, as the electrifying voice of Michael O'Hehir came over the air and lit up the great gatherings. There was never another Michael O'Hehir. It was said that, even when a match was dull, he'd have people sitting on the edge of their seats. From the moment he led off with: 'The whistle! The throw in! And the game is on!' until he finished with 'and there goes the full time whistle!' the listeners were in paroxysms of excitement.

But let me get to what I really want to talk about. Tom had fought in World War I – was wounded at the Somme – and I was really curious about his experience in that slaughter-house. But he never wanted to talk about it. Having read Birdsong, I now know why. We are dealing with a wasteland of blasted trees, slimy trenches and a no-mans-land strewn with the corpses of numberless young men ruthlessly scythed down in the first bloom of youth. Is there a better description of hell? How could the world ever let it happen? Inexplicably, how is it still happening? Cannot humankind evolve beyond this barbarity? In the end, these conflicts can only be resolved by dialogue. In God's name why not start with dialogue?

In my questions to Tom, I was, of course, only being a curious kid, nourished on thrillers like *The Fighting 69th*, starring Pat O'Brien and Jimmy Cagney. I had seen it with all the other howling children at a Sunday matinee in Bill Egan's cinema in Ballybeg. This curiosity led me to unthinkingly ask on one occasion: 'Tom, did you kill any Germans in the war?'

I guess he was taken aback, yet he gave no sign of it. After a long silence he replied quietly, 'Ah you wouldn't know.' Then, after another lengthy pause, he went to the dresser, stood on a chair and got hold of a tin box that rattled as he stepped down. It was by no means in pristine condition – had seen sterling service.

I waited eagerly as he opened it. Inside were various knick-knacks: medals, insignia, a pin with a German cross, like those you'd see on their aeroplanes. From these he singled out a huge, thick brass medal. On one side there was the image of Jesus, on the other Mary. He pointed out something to me that didn't really

INCIDENT BY THE SOMME

need pointing out: a veritable trench had been cut by a bullet across the figure of Christ. And the brass in the trench shone more brightly.

'It saved your life,' I said.

'Yes, I wore it on my chest. The bullet glanced off it and wounded me.'

He put the medal carefully in its box and placed it back on the top of the dresser.

I knew that Tom had been wounded in the war. All his life, he wore a support round his midriff. Despite that, he was active in politics, a great supporter of Jimmy Pattison (father of Seamus) of the Labour Party. At Jimmy's request, he ran, unsuccessfully, for the local Kilkenny County Council. I never felt he was ruthless enough to be a politician.

Regarding the medal, I didn't ever forget the incident, but I spent many years out of Ireland and it slipped to the recesses of my mind. During those years, Tom and Bridie passed away. On my return, I began to wonder as to the whereabouts of the precious souvenir. I asked Tom and Bridie's son if it was still treasured in the home. To my astonishment, he had never heard the story or seen the medal. Nor had any other member of the family whom I asked. But that was Tom – a modest soul. What became of the medal? Was it just disposed of in a spring cleaning by someone who didn't appreciate its significance? Or did Bridie quietly slip it into Tom's coffin when he died? I'd dearly love to know. However, I probably never will now.

Out of this World

The young monk had a vertigo problem and it was decided that he must leave his strictly enclosed monastery and visit a GP. Dr Murphy was a big bluff man but not too well acquainted with 'the ins and outs' of monasteries, least of all with their language usages.

When the shaven-headed Brother Aquinas presented himself in his grey monastic garb with its cowl and cord round the tummy, the good doctor greeted him kindly. He asked him a variety of questions, among them ones about his diet. There was nothing fancy about it, just wholesome organic vegetables and homemade soups. He mentioned that, for breakfast, there was usually Quaker Oats.

'That's very broadminded of you monks,' said Dr Murphy with a hearty laugh. 'And do you get a good night's rest?'

'We retire at 9 p.m.' said Aquinas, 'but I'm always wide awake at 2 a.m.'

'Oh, how come? You can't be having prostate problems at your age.'

'No. I don't have any problem with that less noble part of the body,' replied the young Aquinas, modestly casting his eyes down.

Dr Murphy looked at him in surprise, 'What do you mean 'less noble part of the body'? Just you try going without it, brother.'

'I was under the impression, doctor, that a prostate can be removed.'

'So can a leg. Nevertheless it's preferable to hold on to it.'

'A bell summons us to prayer at 2 a.m.' said Aquinas to explain the nocturnal rising.

'I must talk to the abbot about changing that to a more reasonable hour.'

'I don't think he'll listen,' replied Aquinas with an enigmatic little smile.

'Why not?'

'The monks have been doing this for hundreds of years.'
'Well, it's never too late to learn,' said Dr Murphy.
'Get behind me, Satan!' said the young monk.
'Who are you talking to?'
'Myself.'
This vertigo is having some ill effects, thought Dr Murphy.
As he proceeded to examine Aquinas, he noticed a little red mark on his arm. 'What's this?'
'I administer myself the discipline.'
'You mean you beat yourself!'
'Yes.'
'When I was at school, someone administered it for us.'
'Not the same. No merit. You took it unwillingly,' explained Brother Aquinas.
'Oh, you're right there. I must admit we weren't gluttons for merit.'
When the doctor had finished examining Aquinas, he asked a final question: 'Did you ever have this complaint before?'
'Well, I did have a little touch of it once before, when I was in the world.'
The wide-eyed doctor looked at him utterly perplexed. 'As a matter of interest,' he enquired, ' where the heck do you think you are now?'
Feeling that any attempt at an explanation would baffle the good doctor, Aquinas just smiled seraphically and remained silent.
'You were about to say?'
Aquinas went on saying nothing – seraphically.
'Well, it doesn't seem as though I'm going to get an answer to that query,' the doctor finally observed.
'It's just that I have been figuring out an appropriate reply, doctor. The best I can do is to say that I am in the world but not of it.'
'As far as I can see you're very much in it and of it.'
Brother Aquinas just sighed.
'How's your love life?', asked the doctor having recourse to a little shock therapy to elicit a response.
'I find cold showers very effective for calming the passions.'
'Cold showers!?'

'Only kidding, doctor. I do think we should have more dialogue about the facts of life though.'

'Isn't that a question of intercourse rather than dialogue? But let's get back to your health.'

'Where my health is concerned, I'm resigned to whatever comes my way.'

'It may be so but I am faced with the task of keeping upright this monk who stands before me, so I am going to prescribe some tablets and recommend that you skip the 2 a.m. prayer for a spell … Do you monks produce any beverage like Benedictine or Buckfast wine in your monastery?'

'Sadly no,' announced Brother Aquinas.

The doctor noted the word 'sadly'. There was hope for this young fella. 'Well, if you can get your hands on either the Benedictine or the Buckfast, take a tot before you go to sleep; it will do you all the good in the world. And tell the abbot, it's a strict order!'

This time Aquinas just smiled seraphically once more. Satan wasn't ordered to go anywhere.

'Any questions?' asked the doctor finally.

'Just one.'

'Yes?'

'How can a monk remain upright when his doctor orders him to drink Buckfast wine and Benedictine?'

This rookie monk was full of surprises. 'Why not get Father Abbot to join you in the toast, so that he can grab you before you topple over.'

Brother Aquinas was really tickled by this suggestion and got into an incontrollable fit of the giggles.

In the interim, Dr Murphy checked his watch and suddenly remembered the people still waiting in his ante room. He summoned his nurse assistant and whispered to her, 'Get this young man out of here before I have an attack of vertigo myself!'

Weaver of Yarns

Old Dick Kelly of Ballybeg was the most captivating storyteller I ever heard. No one glued me to my seat with their tales as he did. It wasn't only that, but also the respect he showed you as a child while spinning his enchanting yarns. You seemed to be important to him, which does wonders for a young person's image.

He was an ex-soldier from the British army, had fought in World War I and served in India. Somewhere along the road, he had lost an eye and wore a black patch over the empty socket. This gave him a sinister, piratical look, yet Dick was anything but sinister; in reality he was a lovely man with a soldierly cut and upright mien that defied his advanced years.

Kilkenny hurling was his passion and his stories about the prowess of Kilkenny hurlers were endless. Hurling is a Gaelic game played with sticks, like hockey, and is the fastest field game in the world. A sport without compare. Players can score goals by shooting the small leather ball, called a sliothar, into the net as in hockey or football. The side posts of the goals, however, extend upwards, as in rugby, and, if a player puts a ball over the goal bar, yet between these uprights, it counts as a point. It doesn't matter how high the ball is as it sails through these uprights, once the umpires decide it has passed between them. Three points are equal to one goal. Games are resolved on goals and points, so 1–10 beats 1–9. Barely!

I give the foregoing information in order that the uninitiated may appreciate one of Dick's most dramatic tales. At this point, I will allow him to take up the story. Things got confused sometimes as he dipped into the potpourri of memories, but that was a trifle. The story was the thing.

> I was above [Croke Park, Dublin] in '35, I believe it was, and 'twas a terrible excitin game altogether. Croke Park was a heavin sea of Kilkenny black and amber and Limerick green

and gold. A hundred thousand people were on their feet roarin and millions more roared round their wirelesses. There was a minute to go and weren't Kilkenny down be two points. Limerick were sure they had us bet. I was shoutin me head off. Didn't a Limerick woman look round at me and, says she: 'Go on wid yer ould mournin colours!' Mam, says I perfetic-like, unless I'm greatly mistaken, the city of Limerick could be in mournin shortly.' [Dick now transfixed me with his remaining eye, so I knew the denouement was coming.] And just then didn't the bould Lory Meagher from Tullaroan get the ball. With eagle eye he picked out Paddy Whalen movin into space down in the forward line and sent him a long, inch-perfect ball. The referee put the whistle to his lips. This was going to be the last stroke of the game. Paddy was somehow in the clear. I think he even had time to shpit on his hands. He grabbed the ball. Took a quick look at the goal. A number of players blocked the way to it. But didn't Paddy hit the *sliotar* an almighty puck and buried it in the net. I believe the force of it carried the poor goalkeeper who tried to stop it into the back of the net as well. The roar that day was heard on the Great Wall of China. Kilkenny had won a great All Ireland by a solitary point after an hour's titanic struggle. Afterwards I turned to the woman I had been arguing with and we shook hands [Dick, ever the gentleman!] and I wished her well for the future and sure, if me memory serves me rightly, Limerick won the following year. There's always a great spirit among the rival fans in hurling.

I was up again in '39, [Dick, warming to his subject.] That became known as the 'Thunder and Lightning Final' and was one of the greatest ever. The clouds glowered over Croke Park and were riven again and again be lightning. With thunder clashin, lightning flashin and rain cascadin down Kilkenny beat a great Cork team – again be a solitary point. The ball flew up and down the pitch at a terrible rate – end to end stuff it was, as the lead changed from one team to the other umpteem times. They say Jimmy Kelly from Carrickshock got the winnin point that came in the dyin seconds of added time. Such was the confusion caused be the fierce storm and blindin rain that no one was quite sure who got the final touch. The crowd went berserk. That was Sunday, September 3rd, 1939 and the Second World War was declared on that day. We celebrated the victory in the All Ireland, but dark days were round the corner. That war was to change all our lives. Sure the very next day didn't Guard Kelly come down our street and ask us to block up our windows, so that no lights could be seen. You see the lights would attract German bombers.

We were back in '47. Cork and Kilkenny again. Wouldn't you know it? It was the greatest ever All Ireland. I saw one of the cleverest things I ever saw that day. In the dying seconds, with the sides level, Jim Langton got the ball and pretended to run away with it on a solo run, but cleverly left it behind on the ground. The surrounding Cork players pursued him, thinking he was carrying the ball, which gave Terry Leahy ample opportunity to pick it up and strike it over the bar for the winning point. Croke Park exploded ...

And so the reminiscences flowed, riveting and endless. Mostly about the peerless sport of hurling, but sometimes shot through with war experiences – memories of hazardous days spent manning a machine gun, as Dick and his outnumbered companions tried to stanch the flood of Chinese hordes, pouring through the Khyber Pass. Maybe it was there that he lost the eye.

Sadly, that unforgettable voice is long silenced.

Pity Beyond All Telling

It was love at first sight. He was smitten the first time he saw her on the dancing platform at Ballyline. On holiday from University College Dublin, where he was studying medicine, and, not expecting anything earth shaking, he went to Ballyline in search of a little fun. After the social swirl of university life in Dublin, Ballybeg could be quite monotonous in summer. It was the last place he expected romance to strike. Surely that would happen in Dublin among those articulate and attractive university women. But at the sight of this girl, he just froze where he stood, captivated by her radiant smile, vivacious blue eyes and brunette Botticelli hair.

When the foxtrot finished and she separated with a musical laugh from the hearty farming lad with whom she had been dancing, he was quickly at her side: 'May I have the next dance, please?'

She looked at him – a little surprised, he thought – and said, somewhat regretfully, 'I'm spoken for.'

'Oh,' he interjected; obviously disappointed.

'But I'm free for the one after that.'

'Great.'

He sat out the next dance, but couldn't take his eyes off the comely girl.

His heart melted when he took her in his arms for their dance together and their eyes really met for the first time. Then she looked away and he could feel her gentle breath on his neck. He drew her to him a little more tightly. They both knew then.

'By the way, I'm Brian Harrison.'

'I know.' Every girl for miles around knew this eligible son of a local wealthy landowner. Tall, fair-haired and handsome, many saw him as desirable, but, because of his wealth, quite unreachable. 'And I'm Kitty Walsh. I doubt if you knew that,' she added with a mischievous smile.

'Why do you doubt?'

'My father is a farm labourer. Sometimes works on your father's domain.'

For a moment Brian's face looked troubled, yet he recovered quickly. 'That's no reason for not knowing you.'

The answer pleased her. Maybe she could dream.

Following the dance, he offered to accompany her home.

'I don't think it's convenient,' she said. 'I see you've got a car and I brought my bicycle.'

'I can secure the bicycle in the boot. Where do you live anyway?'

'Cloneven.'

'That's not too far and it's a lovely evening for a walk.' And so it was; a twilit June evening with swallows still fussing in the sky and the wayside strewn with primroses, bluebells, meadowsweet … He pushed her bicycle.

'Life in Dublin must be exciting compared to Ballybeg.' She was eager to hear of life in the capital. 'I was there only once, at the All Ireland Hurling Final with my father. A sad day, because Kilkenny lost.'

'Most of the time my head is stuck in the books. Medicine takes a lot of work. But we do let our hair down at weekends.'

'You must meet some lovely girls,' she said shyly.

'Lightning hasn't struck yet – not there anyway,' he added. Though she was no university student, she noted the addition.

They went on chatting until the pulsing stars began to look down from space. She wanted to know more about 'goings on' in the distant metropolis, shivered as he told her about swimming in the Forty Foot even in the depths of winter, was fascinated by curiosities like the two mummified Crusaders in the crypt of St Michin's, where the only life form was spiders.

'Spiders!' she cried in alarm. 'You couldn't know I suffer from arachnophobia.'

Arachnophobia! This girl is no daw, he thought.

'But if spiders are the only life form in the crypt, what do they live on?'

As he had just been thinking, this young lady was no daw. 'Good question. They are cannibalistic, actually. They eat one another.'

Noting the tautology, with a small hint of a smile she replied deadpan, 'Yes, that's what 'cannibalistic' usually means.'

She in turn told him about her work in Miss Roche's textile factory. About the friendships among the girls working there and all the laughs they had together. She also let him in on the dark secret of some of the youngest ones. How they mixed aspro with fizzy drinks!

'Hardly too serious,' he reflected.

'But they may go on to something stronger.'

'You mean,' he said, 'that, before we know where we are, they may progress from aspro to Mrs Cullen's powder?'

They both dissolved in laughter at the thought of the dark powers attributed to Mrs Cullen's benign concoction.

She told him how she loved to read.

Ah, that explained 'arachnophobia', he thought.

Her older brother, Sean, was a voracious reader and kept passing on books to her. The result was that from quite a young age she was tussling with whoppers like Dickens' *David Copperfield*, a North Country Curate's *Via Dolorosa* and Franz Werfel's *The Song of Bernadette*. As well as that, even in primary school, the nuns did a superb job on teaching girls to read, write and be numerate. You could build on that, even if you couldn't afford secondary.school.

At this point, a soft-feathered owl flew noiselessly by. Startled, Kitty said, 'I must be getting to bed. Factory tomorrow.'

'Can I see you again?'

She hesitated. 'If you want to.'

'Want to! Would tomorrow be all right?'

'Where will we meet?'

'In this laneway, at eight o'clock?'

'Fine.'

They regarded one another for a long moment in the darkness. Then he took her in his arms and kissed her warmly on the lips.

'Night, Kitty.'

'Night, Mr Harrison.'

'Mr Harrison!'

'Night, Brian,' she added with a silvery laugh.

'Who was that you were talking to out in the lane all this time?'

asked her father, who was reading the Evening Herald by the light of an oil lamp, when she came in.

'Brian Harrison,' she replied.

'And I'm Napoleon,' he retorted, as she tripped lightheartedly to her room.

After their initial meeting, Brian and Kitty met regularly and their love for each other grew by the day. They didn't flaunt their relationship, but went for quiet walks by the clear-watered Avonree with its highly visible, darting silver trout. They say the clarity of the water was due to the limestone soil of the surrounding land. Those walks took them through fields carpeted with buttercups, cowslips, daisies… and on through pine-flanked Butler's Grove and by the Furry Knock, where Áine Woodgate once saw fairies at their dancing.

Áine's description of the scene could not have been more graphic: the little male dancers in silk green suits with hats of the same colour and shoes and belts of black velvet and glittering silver buckles. The females wore deep red dresses that contrasted with skirts and caps of white lace. Their gleaming black shoes also had buckles of silver. Merrily, merrily they pranced about to the glorious music of a violin, played by a fairy with his back to her. Suddenly, the music and dancing stopped abruptly. The fiddler slowly turned round as though he felt Áine's eyes upon him and, when he saw her, the expression on his face grew so accusatory that she had to avert her gaze. On looking back, she found that all those little people had disappeared.

Brian and Kitty always tiptoed by the spot in awe so as not to disturb any preternatural presences.

Because she had read so much, Kitty was always a most entertaining conversationalist. Though he knew a lot about the workings of the human body, Brian did not know quite so much about literature. She would tell him of the 'dark satanic mills' of Victorian England as portrayed in Dickens' *Hard Times*, or have him laughing at Sim Tappertit's antics in *Barnaby Rudge*. Sim was convinced that any woman who caught a glimpse of his magnetic eyes would be reduced to jelly at the knees (in reality he was somewhat cross-eyed). Unfortunately, he lost one of them in the

Gordon Riots, which dimmed his lustre. As Dickens noted, he was left with only one eye while the common prejudice is in favour of two. Then there was that talking raven, also in Barnaby Rudge, who defiantly kept on croaking, 'Never say die!' Even in the local graveyard.

Kitty had also committed a great deal of poetry to memory. Above all, she loved Yeats and would quote snatches of his verse to Brian:

> Down by the salley gardens my love and I did meet;
> She passed the salley gardens with little snow-white feet.
> She bid me take love easy, as the leaves grow on the tree;
> But I, being young and foolish, with her would not agree.

or

> I have spread my dreams under your feet;
> Tread softly because you tread on my dreams.

or

> Where the wandering water gushes
> From the hills above Glen-Car,
> In pools among the rushes
> That scarce could bathe a star…

It was following evocative lines like these that they spent their most tender moments together, resting long in one another's arms.

Though their relationship was discreet, nevertheless rumours began to circulate in Ballybeg that Brian Harrison and Kitty Walsh were 'great' with one another. The consensus was that it could come to nothing. Wait until old man Harrison gets to know, people said. She wouldn't be good enough at all at all.

Kitty's own father, Tom, also heard the rumours. So it *was* Brian Harrison who was chatting her up out in the lane after all. He worried for his daughter. 'Kitty, I don't want to see you hurt. He's out of your reach.'

'Surely that's for Brian to say, Daddy.'

'Kitty, you and Brian are young. This thing is much bigger than both of you.'

'Bigger than both of us?'

'It's not the way things are here, child. It's not going to happen. How I wish your mother Maureen, God rest her, were here now to help us.'

Sean was of the opinion that if Brian wanted to marry Kitty that was his business. This, after all, was the twentieth century and the world had just fought a war with Hitler to get rid of discrimination and suchlike nonsense.

'Who said anything about marriage? Aren't we getting ahead of ourselves! Brian and I are not long going out together.'

And there the matter rested.

Stanley Harrison, Brian's father, was also made aware of his son's 'dalliance'. He had a word with his wife, Henrietta, and they decided on intervention, but 'light artillery' for starters.

'I hear, Brian, that you have been seen regularly with one Kitty Walsh, *a factory girl*.'

Noting the emphasis, Brian replied, 'That's true, Father.'

'Well, it's not uncommon for young men to sow their wild oats with someone from the lower orders. This is obviously a passing liaison. We'll say no more about it.'

'But, Father–'

'We'll say no more about it.'

He'd say no more but had made his opposition to a permanent relationship with Kitty quite clear. Brian knew he might find the relationship difficult to accept yet, naïvely as it transpired, felt he might not be quite so adamant. The use of the term 'lower orders' he found distasteful.

Tom Walsh, did not say anything further to Kitty and she and Brian went on blissfully seeing each other.

The only thing Kitty had to deal with was the good-natured ribbing of the girls at work. There was talk of 'Lady Harrison of Ballinasig' and such like, and one of them might curtsy as she walked by Kitty at work on her sewing machine.

Brian suggested that they were, perhaps, high on Mrs Cullen's powder.

As time went on, the love of Brian and Kitty was deepening rather than burning itself out. An alarmed Stanley Harrison resolved that the moment had arrived for decisive action. He invited Brian into his study. Henrietta withdrew from the scene – a sure sign that something was afoot.

'Brian, we talked some weeks ago about your relationship with that Walsh girl–'

'She's called Kitty, Father.'

'Whatever. I trust you are getting over that little dalliance by now.'

'On the contrary, I am deeply in love with her. I'd like to marry her.'

'Come, come now, you're out of her league. Do you know that her father has been an occasional labourer on this estate.'

'Yes.'

'Only a labourer, and you want to marry her! Have you taken leave of your senses?'

Brian was silent for a moment. 'But, Father, I love her to distraction. Surely you understand what that means?'

'Love be damned,' Stanley Harrison was growing angry. 'A labouring man's daughter marry the son of a substantial farmer? In this society? It cannot happen. It will not happen. Hell will freeze over before it happens.'

'It's up to me really.'

'Know this. If you go against the wishes of your mother and myself, even if you are our only son, I'll cut you off without a penny and break all communication with you. You'll be a pariah. I'm serious!'

'You raised me to be a Christian. This hardly fits in with the Christian vision. If this is how things truly are, then this is a false, hypocritical society.'

'Brian, be reasonable. It will never work. It would be as if an American black woman were to marry the son of a well-off landowner in Mississippi. To all intents and purposes this girl of yours is a knacker,' he blurted.

The look of animosity exchanged between the two men showed that, even if forgiveness could be found for the use of the immeasurably offensive term, the memory of it, on recall, would always cut deeply. Brian got up and walked out.

At their next meeting, Brian related the substance of what had happened to Kitty, though he omitted the insulting name she had been called. She listened pensively, comforting her distraught lover when he had finished.

A few days later, there was a knock at the door of the Walsh cottage. Kitty was in her room reading *Gone with the Wind* – coincidentally a tale of frustrated loves if ever there was one. The film had been screened recently. She heard her father say, 'Come in Mr Harrison, I'll call her.'

Tom then tapped on her door and told her she had a visitor and mouthed the words 'Stanley Harrison'.

'Please ask him to wait, I'll be there shortly.'

Meanwhile the two men exchanged small talk about the good long summer and how favourable it was to saving the hay. They wondered too about Kilkenny's chances now that they had got through a tough Galway team in the All Ireland Hurling Semi-Final. Seanie Duggan was, they agreed, a superb goalkeeper.

Kitty entered and, despite himself, Stanley Harrison got to his feet and greeted her. This girl oozed dignity and self-confidence and, he had to admit, was surpassingly beautiful. She obviously affected people in unexpected ways. Tom retired. She took a seat and looked steadily at him, waiting for what he had to say.

'You probably know why I'm here,' he began quietly. 'It's about your relationship with my son, Brian.'

She remained silent, so that he had to elaborate further.

'You know that we Harrisons are an old and respected family. And, not to make too fine a point of it, it is imperative that Brian marries into a good family too. You see–'

'Excuse me Mr Harrison, but I don't understand.'

'Don't understand what?'

'What you mean by 'a good family'. Surely you mean people who are morally good. We know from our history that there were some so called "good" families that were anything but good.'

'Miss Walsh' – again he said this despite himself – 'I see that you are far from being naïve; you must know that in present-day Ireland, when we speak of a 'good family', we are talking of a wealthy one.'

'Oh, I'm young and naïve really. I dared to hope that things might be beginning to change.'

'Maybe in the distant future. But for now the social norms are written in stone. Brian can never marry you, Miss Walsh. His doing so will bring social isolation for him and for you. He'll be cast out from his tribe – there is nothing more painful than that – and you will share his lonely isolation. You would be too small a nucleus to survive that.'

'Then God save Ireland,' was all that the girl said.

'Miss Walsh things being as they are, there is no alternative for you but to separate from Brian. In this packet you will find a substantial inducement to help the process.' He reached towards her with an envelope.

'No, thank you, sir. It was never about money.'

'Very well then. I hope you will see the inevitability of the situation.' He stood. 'Good day to you, Miss Walsh. I wish you the very best for your life.'

As he went out, Mr Harrison proffered the envelope to Tom. 'I offered this to your daughter to ease the situation, but she declined it.'

Tom drew himself up to his full height. 'Mr Harrison, we are poor, but we have our pride. No, thank you.'

Harrison had been given a few surprises.

Kitty went to her room and cried inconsolably until she exhausted her store of tears. Tom put a protective arm round her shoulder to comfort her. 'I wish your mother Maureen, God rest her, was here. She'd know what to do.' Soon afterwards Sean came in and added his words of solace.

All that night, Kitty tossed and turned and could not sleep. Her mind was too active. She was coming to realise fully the depths of the taboos around her. Maybe happiness would be impossible for Brian and herself given the prevailing social climate. Maybe his love for her would only bring him an ocean of troubles. If this was so, perhaps the most loving thing she could do would be to move off the scene. As the sleepless night crawled by, these thoughts grew and grew. And it all began with a carefree dance, she lamented.

The long summer was now yielding to the first brush tints of autumn. The scene with his father and news of his also accosting Kitty put Brian under an unbearable strain. Then came the shock – he had a nervous breakdown. Instead of returning to university, he was rushed to St John of God Hospital in Dublin.

As soon as she could, a distressed Kitty secretly took the train to Dublin to see Brian. Since it was only the second time she was ever there, she found it quite bewildering. However, she managed to find her way to the hospital. The Harrisons never imagined that a simple girl from a small rural town could be so adventurous. Even so, they had left strict instructions that only relatives were to see their son. 'I'm his sister,' she told the receptionist, with the mental reservation that all Christians were sisters and brothers!

On seeing her, Brian was overcome with tears They hugged and kissed and she sat long and held his hand. He tried to apologise for his father's intrusion into her life, but was quite scattered and unable to concentrate. She told him not to worry about it and talked rather about the never-to-be-forgotten summer they had together. He asked her to recite the lovely poem about the salley gardens, which she did, all of it, from memory.

Eventually a nurse came and said that it was time for him to rest. She did it apologetically, seeming to recognise what was really going on. Kitty tore herself away. Not before warning him not to mention her visit to anyone. She promised to return.

Needless to say, there was no returning to university for Brian that autumn. And true to her word, every few weeks, Kitty went surreptitiously to Dublin to see him. Nurses at the hospital seemed to intuitively understand the situation and remained silent about her visits. As far as the receptionist was concerned, she was a sister! 'Never have I seen such a loving pair of siblings!' one of the nurses remarked to her. And they both smiled – conspiratorially. As for Kitty, she was delighted to see Brian gradually mend.

By the beginning of January, he felt well and was looking forward to being allowed home in February. Early in January, Kitty came to see him once more. He told her of his plans to get back to his studies. He longed to be a doctor because of the opportunities it offered to help people and relieve suffering. And, above all, he was looking forward to life with her and having a family. About the present difficulties with his own family he was sanguine – it seemed to flow from his feeling physically better. Everything will be all right, he assured her. When it was time to go, they shared a kiss that looked as though it would go on forever. A passing male nurse jokingly called out: 'Break!' and all three laughed. 'Goodbye, Brian!'

'See you soon!' and he waved as she went through the door.

Kitty knew that things would never be all right and going out from that place she wept bitterly.

Ten days later, a letter came to the hospital. He recognised Kitty's handwriting and opened it eagerly:

Dear Brian,
Over the past few months, I have thought about our relationship. I have been in agony. Sadly, I have been forced to accept what your father said: there is no chance for us. We were born into the wrong place at the wrong time. Maybe in the distant future lovers will not have to suffer what we did. Darling, if I married you, we would be totally cut off, especially you. Though I love you more than anything in the whole world, I cannot cause you that pain. Believe me, it's because I love you more than anything in the whole world that I cannot bring myself to cause you that pain. Nor do I feel I can expect you to come into what for you would have to be perpetual exile. I don't want to hopelessly complicate your life. Please go on and be a good doctor. By the time you read these words, I'll be on a boat to Australia ...

An unbridled howl rang through the hospital. Nurses scurried to Brian's bed. 'He's having a fit', one of them opined. Wrong diagnosis. It was a heart-breaking.

***

With aching breast, Kitty was on that boat to Australia. Even before she met Brian at the dancing platform in Ballyline on that fateful June evening, she was thinking of emigrating to Australia. Prospects for gainful employment in Ireland looked slim. There was a subsidised scheme that allowed people emigrating to

Australia to travel steerage on a cargo ship for ten pounds. Depleted of citizenry by two World Wars, the Australians were trying to build up their population once more. But the three-week journey out was horrendous, as indeed it had been for so many Irish historically. The food was so scarce and vile that she often went hungry, the ship ran into some rough seas and the crew were fighting among themselves. If she had accepted Harrison's offer of money, she reflected, she could have made this journey in comfort aboard a regular liner, instead of enduring this torment. However, she had no regrets on that account.

When the nightmare of the journey ended, Kitty settled in the gleaming city of Perth, by the Swan River. She quickly got a job in a factory, but, having a secret desire to become a teacher, also enrolled in night classes.

With time, she did indeed become a much-loved teacher and settled into life in her new home. For the remainder of that life, never a day passed that she did not fondly think of Brian and pray that he would find normality and peace.

As for Brian, he never did return to university. Rather he took up farming on the extensive home property, which did not displease his father. Less pleasing was the fact that he 'moped about' and showed no sign of marrying. He never could get Kitty out of his soul.

In the hope that the unhappy young man might find a good woman, Tom Walsh let the word out that Kitty had married in Australia. It was a white lie. Yet it made no difference. Tom eventually died, and so did Stanley and Henrietta Harrison. Brian never married. He pulled himself together somewhat and, apart from his farming, devoted himself to the local GAA club. He felt a need to bring happiness to the lives of young people. He heard of how Kitty had become a teacher and felt she would approve of his enriching the lives of the young.

Believing that she was married and had a family, he didn't feel he could intrude upon her life. As he grew old, however, he eventually did venture to write. A notebook was found among the now deceased Sean Walsh's possessions that contained a current address for his sister. It was headed simply 'Kitty' and gave details of a nursing home in Perth. It was a simple letter which said he hoped she was well, that she was always in his thoughts and prayers and would she please greet her husband and family on his – an old friend's – behalf.

By the time the letter, unfortunately sent by surface mail, arrived at the nursing home where Kitty was a resident, she had died. Like Brian, she too had grown old and their generation was moving on. The letter ended up on the desk of the matron in charge of the home. That lady opened it in case it revealed any business that needed attending to. She answered it:

> Dear Mr Harrison,
> Thank you for your letter which arrived at the above address today, 25 May. Seeing that you were a friend of our beloved Catherine, it gives me great sadness to inform you that she passed away a couple of months ago. Her final illness was mercifully short and she received all the ministrations of the Roman Catholic Church from our chaplain, Fr O'Malley. One statement in your letter surprised me; it was the one about her husband and family. She never married, you know …

When the letter arrived by airmail ten days later and Brian saw the Australian stamp, he could hardly contain himself. He held it in faltering hands and was filled with mixed emotions: delight, trepidation, expectancy … He did not open it. This was a special occasion. Putting the missive in the inside pocket of his coat, he donned his cap, got his blackthorn stick and left the house. He walked through the meadows leading towards Butler's Grove. The waters of the Avonree were murky nowadays and many of the trees in the grove had been cut down. On he walked until he reached the Furry Knock and the spot where the fairies danced for Áine Woodgate a century before. This place had hardly changed a whit and it was a glorious day. With trembling hands he tore the letter open and, to the sound of bird song and scent of wild flowers, read it slowly.

When he, at last, looked up from the letter, his eyes were blinded with tears. Kitty had never married. She had remained true to him – and he to her. Guessing at his intentions, he thought ruefully, if

PITY BEYOND ALL TELLING

without bitterness, of Tom Walsh's white lie. A postscript in the letter referred to an enclosed card that Miss Walsh always kept by her bed. Perhaps it might mean something to him and he might like to have it. He opened the card and, not surprisingly, read:

A pity beyond all telling
Is hid in the heart of love.

Yeats once more. 'Pity' indeed. A tragic tale of lovers, whom God intended to be forever one, cruelly torn apart by blind prejudice.

Other Days

Callers

Having completed her morning ablutions and dressed, Miss McAnally still shuffled comfortably about in her bedroom slippers. No need to rush, she reflected, since she was no longer a busy headmistress. She had retired and that wasn't today or yesterday. The first thing she did was to put out a saucer of milk for Sammy the cat, who was waiting for it after a busy night surprising birds – she had heard the alarmed stacatto of a blackbird – and rodents and attending to other nocturnal, feline activities. 'Here you are, Sammy, put that inside your shirt and it won't matter where the night will fall on you.' It was a saying of her mother and maternal sayings we never forget. All our lives they come tripping off the tongue.

Next she sat down to her usual leisurely breakfast – a bowl of sensible porridge ('stirabout', her mother used to call it), a medium-boiled, free-range egg and a cup of Barry's tea. 'The cup of tea is your only man!' she declared. Another of her mother's mantras. Mother was a prophet, she recalled with a laugh, because, since she herself never married, the cup of tea had in fact been her only man all through life. She had been married to St Mary's Primary School.

She washed up the breakfast things, sauntered to the door to pick up the morning paper and then sat comfortably in an armchair by the gas fire with its cunningly simulated lumps of glowing coals to peruse it. In this activity she was totally absorbed and didn't feel the time pass. When she eventually looked at the grandfather clock that stood closely by, she gave a start. 'Lordy, Lord,' she declared, 'the day is gone and I've done nothing. When I was teaching, I would have done a thousand chores by now. Where does the time go?'

Then, as if on cue, ding dong went the doorbell.

She had just returned from Our Lady's Shrine at Medjugorje a few days before and, still full of the joys of the Spirit, hurried to expansively throw open her door to humanity. Momentarily, she forgot her whereabouts.

Three men in balaclavas burst in and stuck revolvers in her face. 'Hit the fuckin floor!' yelled one of the assailants harshly.

Miss McAnally, a little lady that looked eggshell frail, defiantly stood her ground. 'What's this all about?' she demanded.

'We'll ask the fuckin questions, just do as you're told.'

'There will be no bad language in this house!' Miss McAnally was prim and peremptory.

The gunmen were thrown aback for a second ... 'Bad language me ar–'

'Just a minute, just a minute,' intervened the obvious leader of the group, 'Cool it! Come on now, lads, an' cut the bad language. What's come over ye all? ... Now, ma'am, that's an' end to the cursin but I have to ask a favour of you.'

'And what might that be?'

'I need to borrow your car. Could you please gimme the keys?'

'Certainly not. I know only too well what you want the car for. So that you can plant a bomb or shoot people.'

'No, we won't use your car to plant a bomb or shoot people up.'

'How can I be sure of that?'

'I give you my word.'

'I don't even know if you men of violence have any word. Would you swear to it?'

'Yes.'

'Would you go on your knees to the Sacred Heart of Jesus and swear?'

'No problem.'

From a picture on one of the walls of the room, Christ with heart exposed looked benignly down. Before the image flickered a tiny red flame.

The leader sank to his knees before the shrine and with bowed head solemnly intoned:

'I swear that we will not use the car to take life.'

Miss McAnally went to a drawer and without a word parted with the keys to her red Datsun. She knew what would happen if she didn't.

***

'Three gunmen wearing balaclavas today carried out a raid on the post-office in the village of Fordavon, County Tyrone,' announced Rose Neill on BBC Northern Ireland, 'and got away with £3,000. As they escaped, an army patrol came on the scene by chance and opened fire on them. The gunmen did not return fire and no one was killed or injured. A red Datsun, used in the robbery, was later found abandoned near Aughnacloy ...'

Miss McAnally glanced at the picture of the Sacred Heart with its dancing light and fervently thanked God that there had been no loss of life. She stood absentmindedly for some minutes and then called out, 'Lordy, Lord what a day! And it all began by just putting out a saucer of milk for Sammy.'

Daddy, Daddy

Ed and Fiona O'Toole lived near Arklow in scenic County Wicklow on the east coast of Ireland. They were recently married and, as yet, had no family. Greatly in love, they were enjoying one another's company while happily anticipating the patter of tiny feet before too long. It happened sooner than expected, but not as they imagined.

Fiona's sister, Nuala, was married to an American named Errol Forde. They lived in Boston and had a family of four: Fiach aged six, Kieran four, and two-year-old twins Mary Beth and Glenn. Errol was a gentle giant, who had served in Korea, and was worshipped by Nuala and the children. Then, from nowhere, he was struck down by a virulent cancer which took him away in a short space of time. The family was devastated. And Nuala found herself alone in the world with her four small children.

Following Errol's interment, she was faced with a thousand things to do, among them the seeking of suitable employment in order to sustain her young family. The problem was who would look after the children while she dealt with these matters. It was then that Fiona and Ed, who were over in Boston for the funeral, asked why the children could not come back to Ireland with them for a few weeks holiday while Nuala was sorting herself out. Separation from the children, even for a few weeks, was not something she would do if she could possibly avoid it. But there was no alternative.

The plan that materialised was as follows: Nuala would accompany them to Ireland, stay a week while the children became acclimatised and then return to Boston, leaving the little ones for another three weeks. It being May time would also prove helpful; all Ireland became a great flower garden in May.

The children quickly made friends with neighbouring tots, so that, when the time came for Nuala to depart, so engrossed were they with capturing butterflies, that they barely waved her goodbye. It was she who was full of tears.

When the reality of her absence hit home, they missed her, yet they were assured it was only for a short time; meanwhile they would have a wonderful holiday.

And certainly Fiona and Ed made the stay interesting for them. They took them and their new-found friends to Courtown, where they enjoyed the beach and had great fun in the paddle boats. All the children enjoyed a great rapport, though they had their petty squabbles now and again. These of course blew over and left no trace, as they do with children. If only adults could learn that skill. One tiny lad, with a pronounced Dublin accent himself, thought these American kids 'talked funny'. And he was really baffled when Fiach told him he 'was off the wall', or 'out to lunch'.

It seemed that their father's death was not impinging on their consciousness at all. I say 'seemed' advisedly. One day four-year-old Kieran was totally out of sorts. Fiona and Ed just couldn't discover why. They of course asked the lad what was the matter. To which he answered, 'Nothing.'

Then why not join the others at play. He didn't. He just went off alone, sat on a haycock and gazed for hours at the Wicklow mountains. It was odd.

That night, before he went to bed, Ed and Fiona tried again. He really was down, but didn't seem to be able to find the words to tell them why. At last the little fellow burst into prolonged silent tears as though his heart would break. The couple now grew truly alarmed. 'Are you feelin all right, Kieran?'... 'Have you got a pain?'... 'Do you have a sick tummy after all that chocolate you ate yesterday?'

He put his hand in his pocket and took out a sheet of folded paper and gave it to them. They opened it and found a sketch of the round tower at Glendalough and in the right hand corner there was the name of the artist: Errol.

'Where did you find this?' asked Ed gently.

'In the outhouse.'

So that was it. The sketch by his dad brought it all back. Errol was an artist and had spent a summer with Nuala at the old home some years before. He made lots of drawings and this one somehow ended up among the bric-a-brac in the outhouse.

DADDY, DADDY

Now that the source of the hurt had been discovered, Fiona took the lad in her arms and hugged him tightly. Sighing deeply, he calmed down – the tears too seemed to have had a therapeutic effect.

This event had passed out of their immediate consciousness when, some days later, Ed and Fiona decided to take Fiach up Mount Leinster. The smaller children stayed back with a neighbouring family. The scene from Mount Leinster was awe-inspiring. Yet, strangely, it was the thick white cloud that veiled the top of the mountain that intrigued Fiach.

'Is that heaven up there?' he asked.

'Yes, that's heaven,' replied Ed.

Then, quite unexpectedly, the child said: 'If I could go up there, would I be with Daddy?'

'Of course you would,' replied Ed offhandedly. 'But Fiona and I don't want to lose you. We'd be woeful lonely without you.'

'I'd only stay a little while, Uncle Ed.'

'Okay. Tell you what, when we get to the top, I'll lift you up and you should be able to see your dad.'

Ed was big and strong with a shock of red hair and a copious red beard to match – quite a contrast to the svelte, blonde Fiona. He was your archetypical Celtic warrior and lifting Fiach would prove no problem to him. When they did reach the peak, he raised the child into the heart of the swirling wisps of cloud that garlanded the summit, and held him there for a couple of minutes.

As Ed lowered him, Fiona enquired: 'Well, Fiach, did you see Dad?'

'Yes.'

'And did he say anything to you, love?' He hugged me for a long time and then said: 'You're the big boy now. Look after Mum, won't you?'

I told him I would, and he went off that way – he pointed a finger upwards. Then he smiled at me and waved and I wasn't able to see him anymore.

'That was really nice,' said Ed

'Sorry, I was a long time. I said I wouldn't be long.'

In the silence that followed, Fiona and Ed exchanged glances. Then Ed gave his shoulders a who-knows shrug.

***

As for Nuala, she never remarried. Her life was devoted totally to her family and to her work as a personal assistant to a lawyer. Knowing fully the sacrifices she had made for them, the family loved her beyond all telling. On her fiftieth birthday they presented her with a return ticket to Ireland to spend time with Uncle Ed and Aunt Fiona – and their family! – in Wicklow. The ticket was accompanied by a generous two thousand dollars for pocket money. Fiach presented the gift on behalf of all – he was still looking after Mum.

Rachel

Zzzzzzzzzzzz ... Where was that bothersome fly? Nana, acutely conscious of those hairy legs, crawling with ugly microscopic germs, urged her granddaughter Rachel to deal with it. Rachel's younger sister, Jessica, offered her a fly-swat which she waved away.

First of all, she covered some eats on the living-room table with a cloth and then set about catching the fly. She picked up a book.

'Good', said Jessica, 'that should do it!'

Giving her little sister a wry look, Rachel removed her shoes and climbed on to a table, because the fly had landed high on the wall behind it. But just as she was cautiously approaching it, the creature buzzed away and went careering all over the room, bumped off the ceiling and crashed into the window. Nana ducked as it flew past her. Jessica took a swipe at it, which caused its buzz to rise by several decibels. Finally, it settled on a delicate ornament of a little Dutch boy with his finger in a dyke and a windmill in the background.

'Oh dash it,' said Rachel, 'I can't do anything about it there without endangering the ornament.' She then blew gently on the fly and it immediately took flight and sought the safety of the ceiling.

'Smart fly,' observed Jessica. She threw a ball which barely missed the pest.

'Don't throw the ball, Jess,' pleaded Nana. 'It will leave a mark on the ceiling and your mother will kill you. It was she who painted it.'

Panic-stricken, having narrowly survived the ball, the fly gave a repeat performance of what it had done a few minutes before. It careened noisily all over the room, bumped into the ceiling, charged the window and eventually found its way out into the hallway and up the stairs to a window on the landing. This window was always kept open, but, for some unknown reason, it was unfortunately shut tight on this occasion.

'Both of you just stay where you are,' Rachel told her Nana and sister. She then went gently up the stairs with book poised. Nearer and nearer to the creature she crept. 'Now, little fly, don't be afraid,' she whispered. Slowly, slowly she placed the book on a level with the window sill. 'Now, come on, walk on to the cover of the book.' The fly seemed to sense something and commenced to preen itself. 'You're not to blame if those ugly microbes attach themselves to your legs.' Then the creature walked off the sill and on to the book cover. 'Good.'

Ever so gingerly Rachel raised the book. The fly stayed put. Hardly breathing, she crept downstairs. As she was approaching the hallway she whispered, 'Jess, open the front door. Don't rush.' Jess saw what was happening and got the message. Noiselessly, she opened the hall door. Rachel continued her cautious advance, until she reached the doorway. Then she raised the book and the fly soared to the freedom of a sunny July day.

'You know, Jess,' Rachel said, 'a fly is God's creature and doesn't want to die any more than we do. And there was an ancient Irish monk – maybe he was the one who wrote the Book of Kells – and wasn't there this fly that used to mark the spot in the book that he was copying from. I read it in a text at school.' Jess looked at her sister with fresh eyes and so did her Nana and so did I.

Soon after, I also read in a book that the name Rachel comes from the Hebrew and means 'lamb of God', and what an appropriate name, I thought, for this golden-haired, blue-eyed, compassionate child.

A Dire Decision

The black sky was pregnant with snow. But it was too bitter for snow. Around the yard, under watchful eyes, swirled hundreds of people, walking in an effort to keep warm. Upon their breasts they bore the stigmatising Star of David. On three sides the space was surrounded by grim walls and on the fourth by tall bars.

A young, dark-eyed woman moved mechanically with the rest, her face contorted in silent agony. By her side was a six-year-old boy. He had the woman's large mystical eyes and looked out upon the world, fearful, uncomprehending. The woman momentarily raised her own tortured gaze to Yahweh. She then quickly removed the Star of David from the little boy and slipped him through the imprisoning bars. 'Run, son,' she begged.

'Where will I run to, Mamma?' pleaded the six-year-old.

'I don't know, Ben,' she cried with breaking heart. 'But please, oh please, run, *run!*'

And he ran, he knew not where, into Prague's gathering gloom. Most of the swirling mass shuffled forward unheeding of the drama as they walked the treadmill that led inexorably to – Auschwitz.

More than forty years later, I had the privilege of meeting Ben.

Go Not Gently

The girl lay in the gutter. Mike the young volunteer-worker paused momentarily, conscience stricken. His impulse was to pass by. A thousand others would have done so and easily rationalised their action.

After all, she was just another sad statistic among the millions who died yearly of starvation in the under-developed world, and it was pointless getting worked up over one where there were so many. Better to strive so as to stop things getting this far in the first place. Besides there was no telling what complications could arise if one intervened. It was a matter for the authorities really. The police should look into it.

But Mike was not a shirker and his thoughts were very different. Was it to pass by a case like this that he came to the Third World, equipped with a brand new diploma from the London School of Tropical Medicine? Certainly not.

He bent over the girl. She regarded him with dark sunken eyes, shining unnaturally bright with death. He made as though to lift her, but she shrank away from him. Either the prospect was too painful or she may have realised that she was beyond help.

She moaned, and with skeletal arms slowly raised up a baby, which he had not noticed before, from the folds of her fetid garments. He took the infant from her, whereupon she smiled faintly, sighed gratefully and wearily closed her eyes.

The face of the infant moved ever so slightly. If the young mother could not be saved, maybe this tiny creature could be. He would try the government hospital. Doctor Gomes would probably be on duty. He was a good man and perhaps if he injected coramine and cortisone direct to the heart, the child could be prevented from slipping away and could then be given prolonged treatment. It would be costly, but he could contact his Aunt Tilly. She had money.

He almost ran to the nearest bus-stop with his filthy little pile.

People eyed him curiously, even warily, as they made way for him on the teeming street. He elbowed his way on to the crowded bus and even in those constrained circumstances people shrank away from this lad and his evil-smelling bundle.

On reaching the hospital, he rushed straight to Emergency and confronted Doctor Gomes, who was coping with a long line of patients.

'Doctor Gomes, you must help,' Mike blurted out. 'If you administer coramine and cortisone, you may save this baby and then it can be treated.'

The doctor was disconcerted for a moment by this sudden intrusion, but he quickly regained his equilibrium.

'Put the child on the table, Mike,' he ordered. He examined it carefully, then paused for a second and looked compassionately at Mike's face streaming with sweat after his exertions. He quietly announced, 'This baby is dead.'

'What do you mean dead?' Mike shouted out indignantly. 'If you look carefully, you'll see it's actually moving!'

Doctor Gomes gently forced the mouth of the baby open.

With bowed head Mike sank on to a chair and dug his fingers into his unruly dark curls. He sat there, defeated, and tears mingled with sweat dropped upon his enduring blue jeans.

The tiny mouth was full of writhing worms.

Phew!

Fr Joseph and myself were returning to the remote mission station after darkness had fallen. As we drove along, two great luminous orbs, beside a water hole, were trapped in our headlights. The eyes of a deer, I presumed. I had often seen the phenomenon along roads in Africa and it is a glorious sight. This was India and also jungle terrain.

'The eyes of some animal,' Joe remarked.

'A deer, I think.'

'Could be.'

'Will we stop and take a look?'

'I think not,' said Joe. 'It's getting sort of late. Better get back to the mission.'

Next day there was a bulletin on the radio:

We would like to warn all listeners to be careful. A tiger has been spotted in the area. Please be vigilant and stay indoors after dark until the predator has been captured. If you see the animal, report it to the police immediately. Thank you.

Phew! We were lucky not to have contributed to the enhanced luminosity of those eyes.

Brush with Greatness I

I first set foot in the United States in early October 1957. I well remember getting off the plane and gazing up at an unblemished sky that was being dissected by a billowing jet stream. This was not, as yet, a common sight in Europe. I had just crossed the Atlantic in a KLM super constellation aircraft that seemed to have droned on for an eternity. At one point, I had a heart-stopping moment as I saw the engines of the craft belching flames – until a broadly smiling hostess assured me that this was quite 'normal'. I obviously had to revise my notions of normality.

The air pockets too I found disconcerting. For a long or short period the aircraft seemed to be falling out of the sky. Since nobody else seemed to be bothered, I concluded that this was also 'normal'.

Despite these nasty surprises, here I was in New York on this balmy autumn morning enjoying my Columbus moment. In those days the airport was known as Idlewild and Eisenhower was president; I had never even heard of John F. Kennedy. The airport was far from being the sprawling plant it is today. I crossed the tarmac, entered immigration and handed my green Irish passport to the lady officer. 'Isn't that a bit exaggerated,' she proclaimed in tones a soft-spoken Irish person would find too loud. The cause of the remark? At Shannon they had written on my passport in green ink! She then noticed my name and yelled out (or so it seemed to me): 'Eddie! Your cousin is here. Another darned O'Halloran.' Whereupon a smiling Eddie appeared and gave me an animated welcome to the US of A.

I cannot remember every detail of that eventful day, but I soon found myself in a surprisingly confined area, waiting to be picked up. Eventually I got talking to an elderly porter whose face I can still recall. Since I was in clerical garb, he'd noted that I was 'a young sort of fella' to be so arrayed. I explained that I was still only a clerical student on my way to Latin America to get some years of practical experience. 'I guessed you were some sort of rookie,' he observed.

'I beg your pardon, but what is a rookie?'

'It's a baseball term. It means a beginner. Where'd you say you're goin?'

'Latin America.'

'You speak Latin, of course.'

'I know it, but I don't speak it. In fact it's no longer spoken. Nor do I speak Spanish yet.'

He then went on to talk at length of politics in the United States about which I knew little at the time. The word 'liberals' occurred a great deal in his meanderings.

'What,' I asked, 'is a liberal?'

'Gee, sonny,' he countered, 'don't you know nuttin? A liberal is all for freedom. Mrs Roosevelt who went through here a short time ago is a great liberal.'

I thought that woman had looked familiar. So that's who it was. Eleanor Roosevelt, the renowned first lady and first US delegate to the United Nations. And she had brushed by without my realising who she was. She was a large, impressive woman; I can still see her sweeping past like a stately ship, surrounded by her minions as a great vessel is surrounded by tugboats. It was undoubtedly a privilege to even have seen such a historic woman.

During the following week, I took in the sights of New York: the Empire State Building (the ill-fated Twin Towers didn't even exist as yet), the Statue of Liberty and Ellis Island, Manhattan, Broadway, Central Park, the United Nations … The muscles in my neck were jaded from gazing upwards at skyscrapers. I took the obligatory bus tour and was fascinated by an enormous advertisement for Camel cigarettes, featuring a gigantic mouth puffing huge quantities of smoke into the atmosphere. The guide pointed out the home of the film star, Paul Muni, whom I had seen in a gripping movie on World War II; he had a scar on his face that I found distracting. As we went down skid row, the same guide drew attention to a drug addict, seated on a spiked wall, outside a house. The spikes were there, of course, to prevent this from happening, but, as the guide explained, 'The poor guy ain't got no feelin anymore.' The extraordinary thing, I suppose, was that such a phenomenon was rare enough in those days to be regarded as a curiosity for tourists.

St Patrick's Cathedral was of special interest to me. With a tear in my eye, I thought of all those Irish servant girls who subscribed their hard-earned cents to build this fine cathedral. They had left their homeland in the late 1800s, without the prospect of ever returning, to make their home in the New World. The haunting song, 'She lived beside the Anner' captures the plight of them all for me in a couple of heart-rending lines:

> O brave, brave Irish girls, we well may call you brave,
> Sure the least of all your perils is the stormy ocean wave ...

St Patrick's Cathedral is their monument. Sadly, as an American friend once told me, they were not in the prominent places among the invitees on opening day.

I was delighted to see, however, that Blessed Kateri Tekakwitha, the Mystic of the Wilderness and Lily of the Mohawks made it. Her statue is on the façade. It was totally appropriate then that I saw my first Native American in St Patrick's. She had long shining black hair, a typically noble profile and flowing white robes, decorated at the margins with colourful (vivid red, yellow, blue ...) tribal motifs. A band round her forehead held an impressive white and sable feather in place. On her back, she had a pouch that held a selection of arrows as she glided along softly in her moccasins. I thought of all those movies!

When the friends I was staying with heard of all my sightseeing, they amazed me by saying that they never had been up the Empire State Building or over to the Statue of Liberty, less still to the United Nations. 'That's the story of lots of New Yoikers,' they assured me. Apparently, only faraway hills look green, or, as we say in Gaelic, faraway cows have long horns.

Another curious memory I have of that first visit to the Big Apple was how difficult I found it to spend money, which was just as well, because it was extremely scarce. I would go into a diner and carefully choose something inexpensive to eat. I was dressed in full clericals and must have looked somewhat young and forlorn. I guess the waitresses divined my plight, because they repeatedly wrote me out the bills, then took them and said, 'I'll pay it!' They then strode away without any fuss so as not to embarrass me. I loved every one of those waitresses.

Where eating was concerned, those juicy hot dogs that you bought on the street with ketchup and mustard were food fit for the gods. And I hadn't a worry in the world about hygiene.

Over the intervening half a century I have visited New York many times, but that first experience was the sweetest. The cerulean autumn days were as warm as a good Irish summer and to this was added the multi-coloured glory of the leaves and the honking of Canadian geese on Long Island Sound. The World Series in baseball was being played, probably in the Yankee Stadium, and the city was bustling with happy people. The Milwaukee Braves won the baseball that year and the most elated in the throng were those sporting Indian headdresses.

The most abiding memory, however, is of that stately woman who powered through the entrance to Idlewild. A pity I didn't realise who she was at the relevant moment. In a sense she would have known who I was. I knew too that the tallest things you see in life are not buildings – they're people.

Brush with Greatness II

Rosa Parks was the Afro-American lady who refused to yield her seat on a bus to a white man in Alabama back in 1955; an unjust law demanded that she do so. After a long day's work, she told the bus-driver that she was too tired to stand. Later she was to declare that what she was really tired of was humiliation, oppression and injustice. On retreat three weeks before the historic event, taking inspiration from Jeremiah 1:7–8 where the young Jeremiah tells the Lord that he is inadequate for the role of prophet, her preacher made a telling observation. He reminded his listeners that, although they were weak, God could do great things through them. This sentiment affected her deeply at the time, returned to her as she was asked to give up her seat and led to her refusal. She was of course arrested and thrown into prison. Yet her tiny, though iconic, act of protest was the spark that ignited the mighty and successful civil rights movement of Dr Martin Luther King Jnr.

While staying with friends in Washington DC during the summer of 1999, I had the good fortune of attending a reception for Rosa Parks, who was awarded the Congressional Medal of Honour. I went in the company of a girl from Northern Ireland who, I have it on good authority, was the first to interest Bill Clinton in the Northern Ireland issue while he was still Governor of Arkansas. I had just launched a first novel When the Acacia Bird Sings in Washington and this girl insisted on my bringing a copy to give to Rosa Parks. I was understandably reluctant to do this, but the persuasiveness of Rita M. – the girl's name – was too much for me. I could see how Bill Clinton was won over to the cause of peace in Northern Ireland! The poor man didn't stand a chance.

As so often happens with celebrities, Rosa Parks was delayed, so we had to wait for quite a time. The assembly consisted for the most part of Afro-Americans. The hall was a-twitter with expectation, while some of the organisers bustled about attending to last-minute details. One incident I recall vividly. An extension lead was called for and after some minutes a young man came with one looped over his shoulder. With a touch of gallows humour, an elderly Afro-American male with grizzled hair, fading eyes and probably a long memory said: 'Sonny, I thought that was a lynchin rope you had there!'

While continuing to wait for Rosa, I got chatting at length to yet another Afro-American, who was obviously part of Rosa's security detail; we didn't talk of anything earth-shaking, just about the ordinary stuff of life. But we did warm to one another, I felt.

Eventually, there was a buzz of excitement and Rosa entered to a standing ovation. She was elderly, frail and in a wheelchair. There followed the inevitable tributes to her life and work on behalf of civil rights. What stays with me is the image of a red-ribboned young girl who was ever so articulate and well spoken. I saw Rosa look on her with love and I couldn't help thinking that she made such little girls possible. And, then, there was the man who observed facetiously: 'Rosa Parks has already been honoured by God, the saints, the choirs of angels, the great American public and now – at long last – she is being honoured by the United States Congress.' That got the audience rolling in the aisles – only the cliché seems appropriate. Rosa didn't speak; a lady thanked all present on her behalf. Rosa didn't need to speak. She herself was the speech.

When the function was finished, Mrs Parks, as those present kept on respectfully calling her, was surrounded by burly bodyguards, both male and female. There was no way through the ring of steel. I remarked forlornly to the security man to whom I had been chatting how I had a faint hope of presenting Rosa with a book and carried greetings from an Irish friend of hers. But I saw it was hopeless.

'Take a look, man,' he said, 'can't be reached no how. Stay where you are for a while or you'll be trampled on.' 'Bye,' I called. 'Nice meeting you.' He disappeared into the mass. After some minutes, I saw the crowd in front of me part like the Red Sea. At one end of the parting sat Rosa Parks, at the other stood myself. My security friend beckoned me forward. I presented the book to her and greeted her on behalf of the Irish friend. She smiled and said a few gracious words. I found myself awash in a peace that I have found only in the presence of very few persons in life.

Brush with Greatness III

Strange though it may seem, I had another significant brush with greatness on the same day that I had the encounter with Rosa Parks. And it so happened that it was with another Afro-American lady whose name was Betty. Betty who? I never got her surname. As I walked on air from the place in which I had met Rosa Parks, feeling somewhat peckish, I made my way to Burger King for a coffee and quarter-pounder. Betty was a waitress there.

At first I was in such a euphoric state that I didn't notice her. After all, I had just met, not just one of the great women of the twentieth century, but an extraordinarily spiritual person who, as already noted, emanated a deep sense of peace. Gradually, however, Betty's upbeat voice began to impinge on my consciousness. She was circulating among the customers, spreading goodwill wherever she went with a cheery word for everyone. At one table she obviously surprised a girl by approaching with a birthday cake topped with blazing candles. She then got everyone singing Happy Birthday and made a hearty fuss of the blissful young woman. I have, of course, often seen people presented with birthday cakes in restaurants, but rarely with such panache.

Eventually she stood at my own table. 'Hi! And how are you today, sir,' she asked perkily.

'Very well, thank you, Betty.' The name was on her lapel.

'You visiting Washington?' She had detected the Irish accent.

'Yes, here visiting friends'

'Enjoyin yourself?

'Immensely. It's a wonderful place.' Then, unable to contain myself, I added,

'You'll never guess who I've just met.'

'Tell me!'

'Rosa Parks.'

'*Rosa Parks*!'

'None other.'

'Hey man, you a celebrity!' I winced a little.

'Betty to me every human being is a celebrity. You're certainly one. I've seen the happiness you have been spreading in this restaurant. I'm sure you have made their day for many people coming in here. You may even have made somebody's life.'

You will not be surprised to hear that Betty looked amazed.

The small gesture of Rosa Parks had considerable historical impact and its results are justly well known. This is not so with the gestures of Betty. I believe, however, that her efforts are just as significant and there is no telling their outcome. It is people like her, doing their routine best, that keep this world turning on its axis. And mostly they are women.

Brush with Greatness IV

In 1991 a bus-driver called Tom Hyland was playing cards with friends at his Dublin home in Ballyfermot. They were totally absorbed in their game but the television was flickering in the background. It so happened that the programme was dealing with a notorious massacre of innocent civilians by Indonesian soldiers in an East Timorese graveyard. Just as Hitler illegally invaded and occupied Poland in 1939, so did Indonesia invade the newly independent East Timor in 1975. Two years previously East Timor had won its independence from Portugal.

While waiting for a companion who was pondering what card to play, Tom glanced casually at the programme. It grabbed his attention. He continued watching. His companions joined him. Tom was appalled by what he saw and went on to found a group, or better a movement, entitled East Timor Ireland Solidarity Campaign. As East Timor strove successfully to cast off the yoke of the invader, there was no more effective advocate for its cause than East Timor Ireland Solidarity Campaign.

Tom was an unlikely hero. He says of himself that he used to drive past the US Embassy in Ballsbridge on his bus route and see people protesting outside over various issues. He thought they were 'wacko'. But then he saw priests and nuns among them and it set him thinking: if priests and nuns were protesting about something, there must be a good reason for it. Consequently, when he saw that defining programme, he didn't say, 'Somebody should do something about this', but rather, 'I should do something about this.' The little he could do he did by starting the solidarity group. You could say that he paused in his card game and history held its breath.

Although I admired Tom Hyland hugely, I knew him only slightly. I was amazed at his skills in dealing with friend and foe alike in his pursuit of justice. He came across as a reasonable and decent ordinary man who treated all with respect. I had no idea that our paths were going to cross briefly, yet significantly.

***

The people of East Timor were threatened with genocide at the hands of militias opposed to their independence from Indonesia. So the media reported. It was Saturday 11 September 1999. I stood appalled in my office. 'This can't be!' I thought. 'Somebody has to do something.' There followed a disturbing question: Why not me? Predictably there were the rationalisations. What could an ordinary person like myself do in the face of such calamities? It was up to big international players to act. They should really do something about this unfolding tragedy. But conscience went on troubling me. There must be something you can do yourself, however small, it urged.

Then I thought of the All Ireland Senior Hurling Final that was being played the following afternoon between Kilkenny and Cork. I was an ardent Kilkenny fan and had a marvellous ticket for the Hogan Stand and had rushed back from abroad to be present. If I got involved in the East Timorese issue, I might well end up having to give the All Ireland a miss. Every hurling fan lives each year in the hope that their team will be in the All Ireland, and win it. It's a raw tribal urge. Imagine the torment I went through. My nobler part conquered, however, because, when it became an issue of attending the All Ireland or saving lives, there could, realistically, be no contest. If I were to miss the final, so be it.

Yet the question as to what to do still remained. It was then that I thought of Ann Edwards. Ann was President Clinton's Advance Press Secretary and I had met her on a visit to Washington in 1996. I was spending time with Adrian O'Neill, his wife, Aisling, and children, Tomás and Aoife. Adrian was a diplomat at the Irish Embassy in Washington and, through Ann, organised a White House visit for me. Ann herself kindly showed us round and treated us to soft drinks in her office afterwards. I then had a conversation with her, which gave me a chance to get to know her better. I found her a most friendly person.

And so it was on that fateful night of Saturday 11 September 1999, the thought suddenly came to me: Why not phone Ann Edwards? I had read in the media that East Timor Ireland Solidarity Campaign had been urging the United States and others to intervene on behalf of the East Timorese. Before trying to ring

Ann I felt I should call Tom Hyland, the founder of the organisation. Luckily, Tom was available. It wasn't always easy to track down such a busy man. I found him quite downhearted. The latest news from East Timor was bad. The militias that supported Indonesian occupation were killing people. Some of them had even managed to enter the United Nations Compound in Dili and shot people being harboured there. Tom had also received a call from an East Timorese friend of ours, José Belo, a relative of Archbishop Belo; José was in the United Nations compound and rang – to say goodbye. He didn't expect to come out alive from that place. Tom urged him not to lose hope; we would do our best to get him out. He replied that even if he wanted to he couldn't leave because his wife and child were there with him. I then told Tom about my idea of phoning Ann Edwards. He eagerly encouraged me to do so and mentioned that the East Timor Ireland Solidarity Campaign had sent an emissary to Washington, urging the Americans to intervene to save the Timorese. The emissary, however, only managed to see a lesser official in the State Department.

I phoned Ann. The phone rang and rang. If Tom Hyland was hard to contact, imagine how slim were the chances of reaching the even busier Advance Press Secretary of the President of the United States. I was about to give up when a man said 'Hello!' It was her husband, Tom, whom I was relieved to hear say, 'Just a minute and I'll get her for you.'

When Ann came on, we engaged in the customary pleasantries and small talk for a while. Then I said, 'Ann there's something I really need to speak to you about.'

'Oh I guessed you weren't just calling by the way.'

'It's about East Timor.'

'I know, I know, but if East Timor breaks away from Indonesia that whole archipelago could start falling apart.'

'But Ann, East Timor was never a part of Indonesia; it was a Portuguese colony that declared independence from Portugal in 1975. It was invaded by Indonesia that same year as illegally as was Poland by Germany in 1939. Indeed on 7 December 1975 the United Nations Security Council called on Indonesia to withdraw its troops from East Timor.' Ann considered this and, knowing I was a Catholic priest, asked me how the church was faring.

'Archbishop Belo has been exiled and Bishop do Nascimento beaten up. We feel there is a window of opportunity of about a week for a force to go in and prevent genocide.'

At this point I sensed that I was getting through to Ann and I went on to tell her about my friend José Belo and the atrocities that were happening in East Timor as we spoke.

'Look,' she said, 'there are people in the administration who think as you do on this problem. There is in fact a general who shares your sentiments. I'll tell you what. Write a letter saying those things that you have said, fax it to me and I will have it on the President's desk in the morning.'

I was dumbfounded and started-backpedalling. 'Ann, there is a man here in Dublin called Tom Hyland, the founder of East Timor Ireland Solidarity Campaign, he is really the one who should write the letter on behalf of the organisation.'

'I know that you in Ireland are more informed than most on the East Timor issue. Let both of you write letters and I will have them on the President's desk in the morning,' she repeated. This good woman was certainly playing her part.

Once Ann had rung off, I got back to Tom Hyland. Since he was better informed, we agreed that he should compose the letter and we would both sign it. It was written on the official notepaper of East Timor Ireland Solidarity Campaign, which figured a long list of distinguished patrons, and was dated 12 September 1999; it was after midnight when we finished composing it. It read as follows:

East Timor Ireland Solidarity Campaign
24 Dame Street
Dublin 2

President William J. Clinton
The White House
Washington DC

12 September 1999

BRUSH WITH GREATNESS IV

Dear President Clinton,

We write to you as campaigners for human rights from the elation of the independence vote [in the East Timorese referendum] to the despair of recent events.

On Wednesday night, we received a telephone call from inside the UNAMET compound in Dili, the capital of East Timor. It came from a very dear Timorese friend, José Belo. José came to Ireland earlier this year to study peace and reconciliation. He met many people involved in Northern Ireland's peace process in which you have had such a crucial role.

José rang to say goodbye. We told him that we would do everything we could to get him out, but he informed us that even if we could get him out, he could not leave his wife and child behind. We have had no further correspondence from José and do not know if he and his family have survived.

Mr President, as individuals who have been deeply impressed with your involvement in the Irish peace process we are pleading with you to help stop the killing of a most wonderful and gentle people, the East Timorese.

We remember your inauguration on the television and were delighted that you had been elected President of the United States. What will be forever etched on our memories is Michael Bolton's song, 'It's Been A Long Time Coming'. We were close to tears watching and listening, but the knowledge that you had been elected President lifted the spirits of all campaigners for human rights.

Mr President, we ask you and plead with you to intervene and save the lives of the East Timorese people. They have suffered so much.

Thank you for reading our letter.

Yours sincerely,
Tom Hyland (Co-ordinator)
Rev James O'Halloran (Spiritual Diector).

On 20 September 1999 the Australian-led peacekeeping troops of the International Force for East Timor (INTERFET), with crucial logistical backing from the Americans, went into East Timor on behalf of the United Nations to stop the killings and smooth the road to the country's declaration of independence. The military regime in Indonesia was soon to go and efforts were set in train to normalise relations between East Timor and Indonesia on the basis of mutual respect for each other's sovereignty. Tom Hyland believes the above letter played a valuable role in these developments.

The foregoing makes the point that no effort is too small in the cause of justice and peace. From minute mustard seeds great shrubs grow. By the way, I made the All Ireland Final, but Cork beat my team Kilkenny. Still it's only a game (aaarrrgh!). Who was the cynic who said, 'No good deed goes unpunished.'?

Thankfully, José Belo and his family survived.

The Bagman

The overwhelming edifice of the Chase Manhattan Bank, its opaque glass polished by the eerie moonlight, soared towards the heavens. From the entrails of the city, a grate at the base of the structure belched perverse incense upwards towards the crystal idol. The night was bitter.

Seated on the grate was a tattered figure that cowered in the heat of the air that so quickly condensed. A piece of rope fastened the great coat in which he was bundled, and he wore a hat from beneath which long matted hair cascaded down. The face was obscured.

Carmen came, accompanied as usual by Sister Yvonne, to give the waifs and strays of the vast metropolis their nightly helping of steaming soup and hot crisp bread rolls. But where was their clientele?

They spotted the lone man on the grate and approached him. He must have come ahead of all the others and would know where they were.

'Where did you come from?'

For a moment he did not answer, but then said quietly, 'The foxes have their lairs and the birds of the air their nests, but the Son of Man does not have whereon to lay his head.'

A smart ass, thought Sister Yvonne.

He lifted his face briefly and looked at them. The moonlight rippled momentarily on the surface of those dark eyes; the face was beautiful.

Suddenly the two women were distracted by a babble of voices. From all the surrounding streets their folk were approaching for their nightly repast. People whose feet were swathed in rags, people whose bodies were wrapped in newspapers, youth wasted by drugs. And the worlds of all were enfolded in the plastic bags to which they clung.

For a whole hour, Carmen and Yvonne toiled as they distributed the food. When all had been served, they remembered the stranger on the grate and turned to offer him a helping. He had gone.

'Can't have been very hungry,' muttered Sister Yvonne.

Carmen looked around at all those whose hunger had been satisfied and remarked pensively: 'Oh yes, he was really famished.'

Again they looked towards the grate. The sinister vapour rising before the immense idol looked as if it would pollute the whole of creation. There was just one star in the middle of the swirling miasma that steadfastly refused to be obscured.

In Search of José Marins

In the summer of '81, I put a pack on my back and went travelling. Lest any friends become facetious about age, I should point out that it was 1981! For a decade I had been working with small communities in Latin America and was now engaged in sharing on the subject with groups in Africa. Because I was engaged in this project, I felt I would like to broaden my vision further, so that summer I went to the USA, Ecuador and Brazil to see communities in those places.

There was one person above all that I was hoping to meet – José Marins, a man who for many years had been doing work similar to that which I was now called to do. But where would I meet him? His activities took him all over the Americas and increasingly to other parts of the world. He could be anywhere on this planet. The chances of meeting him were slim to none. But I realised that a – hopefully – long conversation with José could be most helpful to me.

While working in Latin America, I had become acquainted with Balty – for Balthasar – and my first destination was San Antonio, Texas, where I was to visit him and sus out communities there.

Balty kindly met me at the airport and took me to see an agreeable pedestrian area by a waterway in the city and then on for a look at the Alamo. I was amazed to see how many Irishmen died there. I also thought of John Wayne and how he also 'died' at that spot. I saw that interminable film on the subject of the Alamo in a Dublin cinema years before and, I must confess, it put me to sleep. It may still be going on …

Balty then took me to his house and, seated there, reading a newspaper was – José Marins! I jest not. Out of all the places he could have been in the world, he was amazingly, and unexpectedly, there. As I suggested with an earlier story, some happenings that are factual are far stranger than fiction. Or are they?

Rendezvous

As I boarded my BA flight in Rome for London, I – or any of the other passengers I suppose – was not expecting anything but a routine journey. And, as we flew along at the usual great height, that was what it was proving to be. The hostesses were busying themselves with their various chores and, having adapted the seating for their purpose, a foursome of Englishmen were noisily enjoying a game of cards across the aisle from me.

Since I had travelled up from South Africa the previous night, I was tired and, when the first Alps appeared, I looked sleepily down on the chiaroscuro patterns created by the snowy expanses and dark ravines far below. It reminded me of an experience I had had years before concerning a black and white photograph of a scene very like the one I was witnessing at that moment.

There was a story attached to the photograph. It was said that two friends were walking in the Alps and, while admiring the panorama, one remarked how it brought to mind the greatness of God, the creator. The second, who was agnostic, demurred and, gesturing to the surrounding scene with a sweep of his hand, asked, 'Where is God?'

'Why, God is everywhere.'

'Ok, then, let me take a picture of him,' said the agnostic and, pointing his camera at no spot in particular in the mountains, he took a photo. When it was developed and you looked very carefully at the chiaroscuro scene, a most beautiful face of Christ emerged. I was shown a copy of this photograph myself and saw it. Not everyone discerned it; I suppose it had something to do with the configuration of the viewer's brain or some such phenomenon. Was it a fake concocted by someone? Could well have been. I make no claims for its veracity. But I do for what happened next.

There was an announcement from our pilot: 'Ladies and gentlemen,' he began, and all pricked their ears. At our present altitude, we will soon run into a storm. To avoid this turbulence, we are going to have to go down to a lower altitude, which we will do immediately. There is no cause for concern; it's a measure we are taking to ensure your safety and comfort. Do make sure your seat belts are fastened. Thank you.' The hostesses moved about to make sure that this final injunction was obeyed. They then took seats themselves and very soon I felt odd sensations in my tummy as the urgent operation of descending began.

Looking out the window, the panorama remained much the same. The sun was shining, the skies were clear Italian. Not the slightest hint of a storm. 'Ladies and gentlemen, it was the captain again, you may be interested to know that we are about to pass over Mont Blanc, which will appear on the right hand side of the aircraft.' As I looked out, we passed within what seemed to me a few hundred feet of the summit of Mont Blanc – our descent had been considerable. I was excited. I took a cursory glance at the card players. Apart from one of them who looked briefly out the window, none of the others were bothered.

I turned my eyes back to the summit. Then I saw it. The snow was gleaming on the sunny peak and, owing to the mountain's shape, there was a deep shadow – that formed a perfect profile of the face and head of Jesus Christ. No doubt about it.

Can I prove it? Well, let me put it like this: if you fly over Mont Blanc, with the conditions that prevailed on that memorable occasion being the same, you will certainly see it for yourself.

Tomorrow is Another Day

'Agatha, could you see where Miss Kitty is and bring her in?' asked Monsignor Patrick McCaffery anxiously.

Agatha ladled steaming snapper soup into monsignor's plate and then left the assistant pastor, Fr Francis Frixone, to look after himself as she went to seek out the cat.

The two men took their soup in silence. But the silence was only where conversation was concerned. McCaffery ate his soup as noisily as a camel ingesting water before a long voyage across a burning desert. So many things about the florid-faced McCaffery irked Frixone now. At first, with his career in mind, he had done his utmost to relate to this unresponsive pastor, even accompanied him voluntarily to Rome on an arduous pilgrimage and done most of the donkey work.

On their return to Kennedy Airport, the monsignorial bags failed to arrive. McCaffery complained at the Pan American desk. The girl attending made enquiries and informed him that, unfortunately, the bags had been left in Rome, but would be procured as soon as possible.

'But I'm a *Monsignor*!' he stormed.

Looking nonplussed, the girl shrugged her shoulders slightly, 'Nevertheless, sir, your bags are still in Rome.'

Frixone stifled a guffaw. That was his first slip. He seemed to find the situation amusing. McCaffery glared at him. 'Ahem ... sorry, monsignor.'

Frixone went on to make other 'mistakes'. It wasn't long since Vatican II had ended and he had some wonderful ideas for putting on a 'sizzling' liturgy. A mime at the offertory, for example. He also encouraged some people who wanted to start a prayer group to do so. What could possibly be wrong with people coming together to pray and do some good? But the monsignor did not consider it a bright idea and how dare he, a mere assistant still wet behind the ears, question an experienced pastor's wisdom.

Neither did he consider it a good idea 'to turn the Holy Mass into a barn dance'.

'Dignified mime, a barn dance? Give me a break, will ya, monsignor?'

'A break,' mused McCaffery later. These young fellows had all the breaks as far as he could see. The seminary was wide open nowadays. 'Liberty Hall' he called it. And the seminarians mixed with women in a 'healthy' way. Whatever that might mean. It was totally different in his times. They were confined behind the walls of St Anselm's and were encouraged to amputate women from their lives. They were regaled with stories of heroic mortification like the one that told how St Aloysius Gonzaga refused to look at his mother's face. And there was Italian-born Fr Picca, professor of sexual morality, who warned students against the snares of the opposite sex by saying that woman should not be called donna (woman), but rather danno (devilment ... imagine!).

Mother of God, was it any wonder that he was emotionally crippled. Agatha was the only woman that he felt any way comfortable with. Passion didn't enter into the relationship when they were younger because, such as it was, the seminary had done its work only too well in turning him into an emotional eunuch. As for Agatha, God love her, she had the Irish immigrant's deep awe for the priest. Now that they were both advanced in years, the relationship, like an old shoe, didn't pinch at any point.

But Miss Kealy, the parish secretary he had inherited at St John Chrysostom, now that was an entirely different matter. How the neat little buttocks and breasts disturbed him even now in his later years. He took refuge in averted looks, which gave him a shifty appearance, and flight. 'Flight' was the old seminary catchword. Where temptations to chastity were concerned, there was no standing and fighting, you flew (or was it 'fled'?) as before a forest fire. Life was further complicated by Agatha not liking Miss Kealy. The resulting stilted conversation between pastor and secretary made her job extremely difficult. He admitted it. Besides, she could be forgiven for thinking that, for some reason or other she couldn't fathom, he didn't care very much for her.

The situation was quite the contrary with Frixone. He greeted

'Caitlin', if you don't mind, warmly each day and on special occasions gave her a most natural kiss and hug. God, how he envied him his ease in social relationships. As for himself, he just rotted alone up in that room watching, for the most part, vacuous television programmes and probably drinking too much.

As a result of the airport incident and the liturgy debacle, an awkwardness grew up between the two men, and the monsignor ceased to address his perplexed assistant directly. And as if being frozen out by McCaffery wasn't enough, Frixone felt that Agatha also grew cool and curt with him and would never use a word where a grunt would do. To his way of thinking, the effect seemed way out of proportion to the cause. He told his confidant, the retired Fr Muldoon, as much. Since being an altar boy, he had a great affection for Fr Muldoon, felt he owed him his vocation. 'Ah, poor ould Pat,' said the sunny-haired Muldoon compassionately. 'The bags and liturgy are the least of it. They are only symptoms of his feelings on the one hand and triggers on the other. He's glarin at ye across epochs. That's the real problem. Frank, the time has come for you to call upon your considerable resilience.'

The soup finished, the two clerics sat in tense silence. McCaffery's considerable stomach gurgled and growled like an active volcano. Although he had had a heart bypass, he couldn't endure the Spartan diet prescribed. Broccoli, carrots, celery and radishes were, for rabbits, he declared, and tucked right back into his ice cream.

After what seemed an age, Agatha appeared with a ginger cat. A great fat thing. McCaffery received Miss Kitty on his lap and stroked her gently. Purring softly, like a Rolls Royce, she seemed to gaze towards Frixone with slit contemptuous eyes. The main course came. Chicken again. Miss Kitty was put on the floor where, for a moment, the legs supported the huge bulk uncertainly. Agatha served monsignor. Frixone fended for himself. Miss Kitty mewed insistently for titbits and was occasionally rewarded from the monsignor's dish.

The two men waited in silence for the dessert beneath an impressive chandelier. Indeed the dining room with its long mahogany table, mahogany chairs with deep red upholstery, wood panelling and tear-drop chandeliers spoke of the days when St John Chrysostom was a flourishing Irish–Italian parish with a bustling rectory served by six priests. But now the sheen had gone off everything. The smoky dullness of the chandeliers and paint beginning to peel here and there from the ceiling now gave the room an atmosphere of faded elegance, which was heightened by all the empty chairs round the table. Indeed McCaffery could remember his predecessor, old Monsignor O'Flaherty, holding court over a full house of residents and guests from where he now sat forlorn. The parish, however, was now heavily populated by Afro-Americans, most of whom were Baptists. McCaffery did his best in a paternalistic way to reach out to his parishioners but admitted that he found it difficult to relate to 'coloured' people. He also found it difficult to cope with the ousting of the statue of St Patrick by that of St Martin de Porres. He was not of course prejudiced, on that he was adamant, but each to his own. The 'coloured' people actually preferred it that way, he believed

As he sat gazing at the fraying paint on the ceiling, Frixone was pondering the enigma that was McCaffery. To be fair to him he had always served his parishioners dutifully in a priestly way down the years. He was an impeccable 'priest'. It was as a human being that he became unstuck, as those assistants who had worked with him well knew. Talk about a street angel! If the monsignor were to speak to him right now, he would of course reply eagerly, but McCaffery never seemed to be able to recover from the accumulated trauma of the 'sneering' at the airport and the 'hurdy-gurdy' of the liturgy and prayer group. But maybe the root of the malaise went much deeper, as Fr Muldoon hinted. Despite everything though, he, the assistant, was ready to swallow his pride and talk to the monsignor. After all, he had his career to think about. He just revelled in the ceremonies and solemnities of the Church. He was also fascinated by its honors and pecking order and in his fantasies would picture himself as a bishop one day. If not a full-blown bishop, then at least an auxiliary. In terms of power, of course, being an auxiliary was often about as relevant as being the fifth teat on a cow. Yet there was no denying it, a bishop was a bishop. For a moment he had a satisfying vision of himself processing out of the local cathedral, scattering triple blessings like confetti on reverently bowed heads.

At worst he hoped to become a monsignor. Monsignors sure looked impressive in full regalia and they usually were pastors, with a power base. So he must play his cards properly, not blot his copy book, not rock the boat – all that sort of thing. And that was why he had to take all this crap from McCaffery, his faithful Agatha and even from that damned snob Miss Kitty.

He felt as though he were trapped in the jaws of a tacit conspiracy. If he could get patiently through this assignment, perhaps the next would be better. Lord, but it was frustrating, not to say humiliating. What was it all doing to his self-respect? What did he not suffer because of ambition? Yes, he was ambitious. He readily admitted it. But it wasn't crude ambition for ambition's sake. It was holy ambition. After all, being ordained a bishop meant receiving the fullness of the priesthood – a praiseworthy goal, surely. And he would use power to do some good. There were those who exercised subtle control over mind and heart to achieve their ends. The manipulation of friends was not for him. He'd be up front or nothing. Besides, the desire to get up there was truly American. 'Excelsior,' the poet had said. It was, of course, a very human desire too. What's the old saying? Oh yes, when ten new monsignors got the purple, a hundred got the blues.

The truth was that nearly everybody was partial towards preferment. Few indeed showed the suicidal tendencies of the much-loved Charlie Swartz. He had to laugh again at the daring of it. Just imagine, the Archbishop at the Holy Thursday Mass of Chrism droning a prayer 'for me your unworthy servant, James, and my assistant bishops, Aloysius and Francis.' Then from the midst of the concelebrating priests up pipes the anonymous voice of Charlie, 'equally unworthy'. Ah, the dessert at last. He had been quite carried away by idle reveries.

So as to allow the food to settle, McCaffery ordained an appropriate lapse of time between the main course and the dessert. Agatha spooned ice cream on to McCaffery's plate and topped it tastily with chocolate. Frixone helped himself. 'Would

Monsignor like some coffee,' the housekeeper enquired. 'No thanks. Come here, my dainty Miss Kitty,' said McCaffery. 'Have you been chasing squirrels?' Picturing the 'dainty' Miss Kitty chasing squirrels, Frixone nearly had to bite off his tongue to stop himself from exploding with laughter. 'Naughty, naughty Miss Kitty,' continued the monsignor. 'And what are you doing tomorrow? You don't know. Well, I'll be saying the 11 o'clock mass. It's Sunday, you little infidel. And what will Fr Frixone be doing, Miss Kitty? Oh, Fr Frixone will be saying the 8 and 9 Masses. This afternoon he heard confessions from 3 to 4. Well that's not quite correct, because you saw him enter the church at 3:15, isn't that so, Miss Kitty? What did you think of that, tabby? You didn't approve! My, but aren't you the organised and disciplined cat and without seminary training too. Maybe you're better off. All they seem to get in the seminary nowadays is liturgical dance, guitars and plenty of old talk about 'self-fulfilment', not 'self-sacrifice', mark you. For ordination, I remember I got a present of a mass kit. Today they get all sorts of machines with things hanging out of them. Ah well, times change. The only consoling thing is that God is unchanging and that's why me an' you must hold the fort, isn't it. Miss Kitty? After all, they may not see our likes again.'

'To live is to change, and to be perfect is to have changed often,' blurted Frixone, unable to contain himself for another second. 'And that's Cardinal Newman!'

'Is it now?' parried McCaffery, surprised by this unwonted intervention. He stood up. Miss Kitty, anticipating his exit, strolled regally to the door with tail held aloft.

'You don't seem to think much of Cardinal Newman's dictum, do you, Miss Kitty?' said McCaffery and followed her out.

Later, monsignor was relaxing with a beer, watching television in the room adjoining his bedroom. Agatha fussed over him. Having removed his shoes, she was now helping him to get on his bedroom slippers.

'How do you rate Fr Spaghetti, Agatha?'

To his satisfaction, she just raised her eyes to heaven in Celtic conspiracy with him.

'Ah sure, don't be too hard on the unfortunate angashore,

Agatha. He doesn't seem to be too happy. Hardly a word out of him at dinner. Poor fella seems to have a communication problem. Which is amazing really, because the seminary is wide open nowadays – to women an' everything. But maybe that's precisely the problem, too much exposure and then these young buckos find celibacy a burden. I've always said meself that high walls are a great assist to celibacy.'

Agatha helped him to light his pipe.

'If he had any sense, he'd ask the bishop for a change. Mind you, I'm not going to do anything to give him the push. I never do in cases like this. They'd say I can't get on with me assistants.'

'Give it time and he'll ask for a move,' volunteered Agatha, well aware of patterns. She usually went along with everything monsignor said. She had been a priest's housekeeper since arriving from Ireland as a demure and prepossessing young girl all of forty summers before. Twenty-five long years she had devoted to Monsignor. Sometimes from an upstairs window she gazed long at the children playing in the park opposite until, at last, sighing deeply she retired downstairs to her childless kitchen.

Having been given his weekend programme via Miss Kitty, as usual, Frixone was back in his own room. The wear and tear of his lack of relationship with McCaffery was beginning to tell. He gazed blankly at a wall. A television set flickered in the corner, yet he paid no heed. This scenario was becoming all too frequent. It was two years since his ordination. For a time he had been on a high. Now, with the honeymoon over, he began to feel the true weight of his commitment. Ahead stretched long and lonely years. Loneliness was inseparable from the human condition whatever the calling, but the priest was forever vowed to a solitary bed. He could literally feel his heart sinking and depression take a grip on him. But then, he shook himself out of his brooding with the realisation that madness lay that way. 'I'll think of all that tomorrow. I can stand it then.' He uttered the defiant words of Scarlett O'Hara, finding that they echoed his sentiments exactly. He had read the novel about four times.

* * *

There was no further tolerating Fr Alvarez, his assistant pastor, the monsignor concluded. He was upsetting the parishioners wholesale with his liberation theology, option for the poor and pacifism. Pacifism, for God's sake, in an area where many gained their livelihood from the manufacture of Patriot missiles. Nothing would do him on his last day off but to go up to Washington DC and protest the Gulf War. It must be enough to drive George Bush to broccoli. There were better things one could do on a day off. Play the machines in Atlantic City for one. The guy was a sucker for punishment. Fancy telling the few who ventured into the parish from exclusive Forest Boulevard to undo themselves of their wealth and opt for the simple lifestyle of Christ. He laughed aloud at the very idea. 'Save yourselves,' says he to those millionaires, 'by saving others. Be content with having enough'. Enough. What was enough? One person's 'enough' was a simple home and job, another's a townhouse, a country mansion and a yacht on the Caribbean as well. Wasn't last Sunday the limit? The delegation that went round to the sacristy to protest his sermon was fit to be tied.

Imagine ironically telling the pillars of the parish to take the gospel and cross out all the bits they didn't like, so that he could avoid preaching on them in the future. True, he livened up the liturgy and was good with groups, but everything was blighted by his bolshy approach to justice. No, there was no wearing this. The poor 'spic' was out of his depth. He would see the bishop and have him transferred, for his own good of course. It wasn't as if he was driving him out. Oh no, he could never do that. Fortunately, the bishop was a sound conservative, recently appointed by Rome. He didn't anticipate problems. However, he would talk to Fr Alvarez before the day was out. He felt he owed him that. He was, after all, a zealous if misguided priest.

'Fr Alvarez,' he began, 'first of all let me say quite definitely that I do appreciate your zeal and commitment to this parish.'

'But nevertheless, Monsignor Frixone, you're going to ask the bishop to move me,' interposed Alvarez.

'Well ... er ... yes,' bumbled the monsignor, somewhat taken aback. 'It's ... er ... for your own good.'

'You needn't be embarrassed, I saw it coming.'

'You did badly upset some of the pillars of the parish, you know.'

'Jesus upset some of the pillars of the parish in his day too.' Countered Alvarez quietly.

'There you go, the typical idealist, speedily grabbing the high moral ground. But analyse your appeal to the people not to have anything to do with the manufacture of Patriot missiles, for example. We're living in times of great unemployment, father. Factories are being relocated in the Third World, where the people have to work for starvation wages. What are our good people supposed to eat? Protest placards?'

'Some of our bishops have started funds to help people who opt out, until they can find alternative employment.'

'Aha, if pigs could only fly! That seems a very precarious basis on which to give up a job.'

'But the bottom line is that it is wrong to produce those weapons of mass destruction.'

'That's according to you. There are those who argue otherwise. If only you could tone down your rhetoric a bit, be a little more careful and reasonable in what you say—'

'Monsignor, I can't do that. It's not that I enjoy confrontation. It's just that I have to say what I believe to be true.'

'That's why I think you could do with a change. Look, you're a young man; this is your first assignment. Allowances will be made for your youth and inexperience. What I'm trying to say is that this may do little harm to your career.'

'Career be damned!' Alvarez blazed momentarily. 'I have no interest in preferment. I'll not sell my soul for a mess of pottage.'

These last words and the emphasis on the 'my' had a devastating effect on Frixone. It was as if a boxer were cruising to a comfortable win on points when suddenly his head is whiplashed with a stunning blow to the jaw. In a thrice the positions of the contestants are irrevocably reversed.

'Who could sell their soul for a mess of pottage?' Frixone struggled to sound casual.

Alvarez was silent.

'Who could do so?' persisted Monsignor Frixone.

TOMORROW IS ANOTHER DAY

Again Alvarez said nothing and his silence was tearing the scales from the old man's eyes more effectively than a million words. Was this how others saw him? As an unprincipled climber? He felt absolutely mortified. 'You owe me an answer,' he said in a shaken voice.

With utter yet lethal integrity, Alvarez replied softly, 'I'm not required to be judge to any man.'

Frixone felt as though his whole insides had been gutted. He was tottering on the ropes. He struggled to rally. 'There's no room for sentiment. You must go. It's a matter of princip ...' But an ultimate honesty was undoing him and the words died on his lips. Totally devoid of conviction, they echoed hollowly in the shell of his being. Of a sudden he was old and lost.

Alvarez silently left the room.

As Monsignor Frixone shuffled towards his bedroom, the housekeeper, Clara Maria, called from the bottom of the stairs, 'Dunna forgot to take you medicine, monsignor.' He looked trance-like at the figure standing below. A quarter of a century fell away and there was Agatha. 'And again the wasted years,' he whispered to himself with a heart full of tears.

'You all right?'

'Yes ... yes,' he said falteringly and retired.

Clara Maria looked worried. 'Is that Alvarez upsettin monsignor again!'

He looked at his reflection in a mirror. The hair was a dull grey and the face had long settled into satisfied and compromised folds. Then he confronted the photograph of himself as a lean young assistant to Monsignor McCaffery. The earnest youthful eyes gazed at him across the years. He groaned. 'Did you get it wrong?' he asked his younger self. 'Was the price too high?'

For what seemed an age, he just stood dejectedly like a dog that had been whipped.

'Frank, the time has come for you to call on your considerable resilience,' a beloved and unexpected voice eventually echoed from the past. Gradually he drew himself up to his full height and cried out: 'I'll think of all that tomorrow. I can stand it then. After all, tomorrow is another day.'